SH!T
BAG

XENA KNOX

SH!T
BAG

HODDER

HODDER CHILDREN'S BOOKS

First published in Great Britain in 2023 by Hodder & Stoughton

1 3 5 7 9 10 8 6 4 2

A CIP catalogue record for this book is available from the British Library.

ISBN 978 1 444 97205 4

Typeset in Goudy Old Style BT
by Palimpsest Book Production Ltd, Falkirk, Stirlingshire

Printed and bound in Great Britain by Clays Ltd, Elcograf S.p.A.

The paper and board used in this book
are made from wood from responsible sources.

Hodder Children's Books
An imprint of
Hachette Children's Group
Part of Hodder & Stoughton Limited
Carmelite House
50 Victoria Embankment
London EC4Y 0DZ

An Hachette UK Company
www.hachette.co.uk
www.hachettechildrens.co.uk

To everyone dealing with their own shit!

CHAPTER 1

'They're calling me Shit Bag!'

My words hang in the sterile hospital air like a privacy curtain speckled with an ominous brown stain.

I wait for Suriya's rage. Morven's rebuke, Neither come.

'The boys are calling me *Shit Bag*!' I repeat. 'Look!' I turn my iPad screen to face them like I'm revealing their Miss Universe scorecards, as they stand before me all dolled up for our end-of-year ball.

This time Morven shakes her head slowly, and the realisation that they knew already makes me gag.

Morven leaps into action and passes me the paper mache puke receptacle.

I dry-retch into it. 'Gu-uhh!'

Suriya has bolted for the door, as far from the potential splatter range as possible – not hugely surprising considering she's wearing a white evening dress.

'Gu-uhh!' The physio warned me about coughing and sneezing. She didn't mention retching in the list of pastimes that'll feel like someone's clawing-at-my-belly-with-a-garden-fork. 'Gu-ugh!' Thank God I'm restricted to clear fluids. If I do finally squeeze something from my shrivelled stomach it'll only be green bile. Though, green bile and white chiffon . . .

'Shall I get a nurse?' Morven says, patting my shoulder.

I shake my head. And accept her tissue to wipe the drool from my mouth and nose. I wouldn't put it past Morven to use the hem of her mum's Lanvin dress to mop my brow. Yes, Lanvin. Really.

'You sure?' Morven says, furrowing her professionally contoured forehead.

I nod and lie back knackered against my pillows.

The girls do a slow-dance shuffle round my single hospital room. Suriya relocates to the plastic upholstered recliner in the corner. Morven hovers midway between the bed and the door, apparently unconvinced I'm well enough *not* to alert a nurse.

Wishing I was just high on their perfume fumes, I close my eyes and say, 'Who started it?' I crack open an eyelid.

Morven winces and bites at her high-glossed bottom lip.

Now the garden fork's at my lungs.

Suriya stretches out red-tipped, dark fingers along each

2

armrest, like a cat about to rip up the sofa with her claws, and says, 'Lockie started it . . .'

'Shut up!' I hug my grey paper mache chunder bowl.

'Told you she wouldn't believe us,' Suriya says.

They exchange this look.

'Fu . . . c . . . k . . . !' I exhale like it's my last breath. I can't believe this. 'How do you know Lockie started it?'

'I heard him,' Suriya says.

'When?'

'Technically, Meathead spread it though,' Morven adds helpfully.

'I'm aware . . .' I hold up my iPad and point sarcastically at exhibit A.

Morven buttons her lips.

'When and how,' I say to Suriya, 'did *Lockie* start calling me Shit Bag?' My voice breaks.

'Oh, Freya, don't cry,' Morven says, patting my pyjama sleeve.

'I'm not . . . crying . . .'

Suriya curls her lip when I use my sleeve's cuff to wipe my runny nose.

Yes, I'm disgusting.

But then she runs her mouth. 'Maccy D's on Princes Street after my ballet exam Wednesday.' She adds, 'I wanted a McFlurry, and Lockie, Meathead and Shawsie were in the queue in front of me.'

'And what?' I snap. 'Lockie just called me Shit Bag?'

Ignoring my interruption, she continues. 'They didn't see me because I was stuck behind tourists. And you know what tourists are like, they're so slow – and I thought I'd ask Lockie if he wanted to come visit you tonight before the ball. So I queue-jumped. But before I could say anything, I heard what they were saying—'

'Tell her *exactly*,' Morven says. 'Word for word.'

'I'm trying!'

I hold my breath.

'So Meathead said, "Lucky escape, mate. Imagine shagging her while she's got the bag. Talk about boner killer." And Lockie laughed. Well, he bit his bottom lip, which is the same thing with him. Then Shawsie said, "She always treated you like shite anyway. That's karma for you."'

Morven explodes. '*Freya* treated *Lockie* like shite? You didn't tell me he said that!'

Suriya jiggles her head, bouncing her dark, blow-dried waves. 'And Lockie agreed – well, he made that inhaling gasp sound that means he agrees.'

Suriya's description of my monosyllabic long-term on-and-off ex is like a fist in my gut. I slump lower, using my bowl as a shield.

'Anyway, the tourists noticed I'd queue-jumped so I had to move back, but then I heard Lockie say, "Shit Bag." And when I looked round, Meathead smacked him on the shoulder and shouted, "Shit Bag, that's it!" And they all burst out laughing. Meathead kept saying Shit Bag over and over like it was comedy glitter. There's no way you can get back with Lockie after this!' Suriya stabs the air between us with a blood-red nail. 'This *has* to be the end.'

Morven folds her bare freckled arms, looking like an unamused yet stylish Merida. 'You should've said something, Suriya!'

Suriya, on the other hand, resembles a bored Jasmine. 'What could I possibly say to stop Meathead spreading *that* round the entire school?'

'The entire school – gu–uhh!'

'Suriya!' Morven hisses. She waits till I finish my dry-retch fest then adds, 'Honestly, Freya, it's not that bad. It's the end of term. By the time we're back in September everyone'll be talking about their summer holidays. No one will remember this . . .' She waves her hand to encompass my body, and swiftly changes the subject. 'Are your mum and dad coming in tonight?'

Dumbly, I nod. But they're not. They knew the girls were coming to see me so they're having a night off. 'You should probably get going,' I say, dragging my mouth into a smile.

Suriya pouts and bouffs her hair as she stands. 'Don't worry, Frey-Frey, we've got your back. I'm gonna give Lockie a piece of my mind!'

'You do that,' I say, and wake my iPad again to stare at Meathead's star post from two days ago – *likes* tallying 378 – of a dancing paper-bag meme with a steaming poo curling out of the top like it's a shitty hairpiece atop the bag's head. Some joker – not Meathead because he's not up to this level of artistry – has superimposed my face on the side of the bag and, in bold print below, my new name: SHIT BAG.

CHAPTER 2

Now I feel like Cinderella. This isn't how it should be, Lockie and me. We should be heading to the ball *together*. Thought he'd at least come visit tonight. Bring me flowers. Say the ball will be shit without me.

If *this* hadn't happened, I know we'd be back together—
Don't, Freya!

Winston's on his plastic chair below the telly. I ease carefully out of bed and creep across the rubber floor, dragging my rickety drip-stand with me like I'm a geriatric Bo Peep. I manoeuvre Winston – heavy lump of stuffed fluff – keeping bent over to protect my tummy from the strain, and nudge him over the bumpers and bars onto the end of the bed. I shuffle back, shutting the door and the light off on the way past, and perch before lifting my wasted legs back under the covers, one at a time, and pull Winston slowly up the bed to join me.

Dad bought me this giant teddy when I was in High Dependency. He and Nibblet have been a tag-team of support over the last couple of weeks. Nibblet's my old stuffed rabbit. I've had her since birth. And by 'he' I mean Winston, not Dad. Though, of course Dad's been supportive. Mum too, in her own *unique* way. But they aren't here to get me through the nights like Winston and Nibblet are. Not here at six thirty in the morning. That horrible time when the nurses change shift and come round to wake you up before they go home. I've usually only just fallen asleep again and breakfast isn't for another hour and a half so why they do it I don't know. Maybe to check we haven't died on their watch. Guess they'd feel pretty stupid handing over to the next team. 'Yes, Freya was up twice through the night so we thought we'd allow her to sleep in before waking her for a wholesome and filling breakfast of clear fluids.'

'Er . . .' says the next nurse come breakfast time. 'Freya's cold and rather solid. I think she's been dead for a while!'

I dunno what it is about this place. It makes you think stuff like that. Morbid. I've even left letters – handwritten ones – in my bedside locker. In preparation. If I do pop my clogs. Morven's one has a list of the songs I want played at my funeral. As for Lockie's letter, I'm tempted to rip it up and write him another. Only, I'm not so sure I want his last memories of his first love – we finally made it official in Primary Four – to be an angry ranting scrawl splashed with snot and tears. Nah. Lockie can read the letter with all the happy memories, full of thanks for always being there when I needed him. That way he can feel guilty for ghosting me and instigating everyone calling me Shit Bag for the few remaining, sad, lonely days of my pathetic life.

I prop my iPad up on the narrow table that niftily slides over my bed and click through to see what the movie algorithm gods are suggesting for my viewing pleasure today . . . *The Fault in Our Stars*. Nice. Positive.

An hour or so later the door opens and I freeze. The overhead light pings on, blinding me.

'Having a picnic, are we?'

Rumbled. I scrunch my nose at Julie – my favourite staff nurse. I got a wee bit depressed during the film. So maybe I threw caution to the wind and scarfed most of the packet of chocolate digestives that Suriya left me.

'Diet Coke?' Julie says, shaking one of the empty cans on the overbed table.

Umm, yeah, so it seems I've drunk two of the four-pack Morven brought me too. This is bad. Really, really bad.

'How are you feeling?' Julie says, stern-faced but raising an eyebrow.

'Pretty good considering.'

'Mmhm. You won't be needing this anymore then.' She reaches over my head and wipes *Clear Fluids Only* from the whiteboard above my bed frame. 'Are you still hungry?'

'Well . . .'

'How about some toast and honey?'

'Yeah? That would be nice.'

'And I'll bring you some peppermint tea. It might help with the wind.'

Oh, bollocks! The wind. 'Julie!' I shout after her. 'Please take these cans or I'll drink them too.'

'If you insist.' She winks and pivots on her Crocs.

The wind. The wind and its inflationary properties become too much about midnight. I don't dare just let the wind out . . . Trust me. Bad idea. And of course I can't sleep. Even with the sleeping pill I get on the late-night drugs round, the caffeine from earlier has me wired. Heck, the sleeping pill wakes me at four a.m. on the dot anyway so it's not like it works. And even if I had slept until four a.m. it would be too late to deal with this situation.

Resigned to the inevitable, I edge my anti-embolism-stockinged foot onto the shiny rubber floor, lean on my drip-stand and steer the wheely Bo Peep crook to the door. I look out into the corridor. There's no one at the nurses' station. I hear a little kid wailing from a private room. The scream sharpens as the door opens and a nurse rushes out and along to the Sluice Room. I wait a moment more, to see Julie speed-walking, carrying a cardboard tray from the Meds Room and disappearing inside to the crying kid.

Julie said she'd help me empty this, but I can't interrupt her now. I'll just have to try on my own. I close the door again.

I wheel to the en suite. Awkwardly. I have a cannula tube stuck inside my elbow, so I have to keep my arm unbent. If you tipped me on my back, I'd look like a zombie throwing the javelin.

Bashing the doorframe, I squeeze inside, and me and the drip-stand back up towards the loo. Hey, at least I know my plumbing's working again. My recent pukeathon, that's extended my time in hospital-hell, started because of a twisted gut. Seems the surgeon was right, painkillers and time *have* unravelled my pipework. Hurray for small mercies! I look down at the measuring jug. I'm supposed to pee in it. So they can check how well this old saline drip's hydrating me.

Peeing's not the plan though.

Just . . . I've not had to do this on my own, and I'm not that good at it yet. But sometimes a girl's gotta do what a girl's gotta do, right? I push my doughnut-print pyjama bottoms down, and my Disney Princess pants. They're ironic.

It's heavy. This *thing* on my tummy. Really full. Ballooned. Maybe I should pull the emergency cord over by the shower? But a siren will go off. Everyone will come running. Nurses will pile into this glorified cupboard. Maybe even that fit student doctor with the big hands and cauliflower ears. 'Hey, guys! It's okay. Go back to your cuppas and Quality Streets. I just need one of you to help me go potty.' Maybe not. I sit down on the loo. Sloshing. Why's it so watery? Will it ever go back to normal? I hoick the hem of my pyjama top up out of the way and grip it with my chin. And fumble with the plastic clip at the bottom. Tense. You know when a plaster's stuck on too tight you don't want to rip it off? In particular if you've not shaved your legs for a few days. You have a choice. Brace yourself and yank. Or have a bath and wait for it to unstick and fall off. Well, there's *nothing* in this situation that would ever make me choose the latter option. Never *ever* would I want any of this to unstick and fall off. Most especially not right now. Bombtastic!

I grip the beige banana clip, right forefinger teasing the catch. Do it. Just don't miss. I check my aim. Close my eyes and hit the trigger – WHOOSH!

You know if you've drunk too much cider and you puke, there's a load of watery stuff that explodes from your mouth like someone's thrown a bucket of cider and maybe a liquidised piece of toast and some mysterious boiled carrot in the direction you pointed and shot? Not chunks, more a marbling of certain colours? Well, that's my view inside the loo's front right now. Or maybe more like the projections after a day of green-juice cleansing. Say I'd drunk kale, spinach and celery juice all day (bleugh) and hurled. I didn't miss. Yay! Life just got so, so much better.

I try to twist on the loo to flush because that'll make this faffy next part a tad more pleasant for me. But I can't because my stomach has a line of metal staples from just above my belly button down to my pubes. And when I move suddenly or rotate beyond a trifling twenty degrees the staple train track causes every nerve in my core to hurt like a psychotic puppeteer has me barbed with fishing hooks and line.

And also because I still have my pyjama top under my chin, an open plastic clip in my left hand and something between my legs that if I do rotate will no doubt slobber on my thigh. No. I have to finish then I can flush.

I prop the banana clip on the edge of the sink and tear off a couple of squares of bog roll. How did the nurse do this again? Still trying to keep my right arm open so I don't crush the cannula inside my elbow. Seriously, this is like some sort of complex equation – if Freya has X in her elbow and Y on the sink and Z under her chin and can't rotate beyond C, what does Freya have left to perform the task? Anyway, I'm holding the tissue out in front of me, taking X into account, and fold one corner into a point. Nope, that's not what the nurse did . . .

Oh, yeah, I curl the point over the end of my finger and take hold of the spouted bottom of the clear plastic bag. I haven't mentioned the clear bag in the equation yet. I should've. Because the equation wouldn't exist without the bag. The one stuck just to the right of my belly button. I don't get why it's clear. As if this isn't disgusting enough! I really don't need to see the green, seaweedy smears inside. And the red— Don't look at it, Freya! Focus on the bag's opening. Keep your eyes down to the bottom. I rub the narrowed end of the clear bag between my first finger and thumb like you do with a new black bin bag. Do they make black bags? Anyway, I get the plastic separated, prod my tissue in the end to wipe around the opening and drop the paper into the loo. I do this two more times, just to be sure it's completely clean. Feeling ever so slightly proud of myself and super accomplished, I scissor the banana clip over the base of the bag and snap it shut so that everything is sealed, watertight.

Yay! Good job, Freya. That went very well! Now . . . I guess I stand up. No, wait, I need to pee. Sod the jug. Yep. Wipe. Stand, feeling light and liberated from the hot-water-bottle weight I was toting on my tummy earlier. Quick wipe around the loo rim with tissue, and flush. Wash. Dry. And pootle back to my bed.

That lot at the ball don't know what they're missing. This is the best night I've had since . . . well, since they rushed me into hospital, cut out my large intestine and stuck a poo bag on my belly.

CHAPTER 3

So now you know. Why Lockie finds me disgusting. And why everyone's calling me Shit Bag. And no doubt you're wondering how *do* you end up with a foul, repellent poo bag stuck to your belly?

Well, it goes something like this. You're doing your GCSEs and, actually, you're feeling like crap. But you're thinking 'nearly done'. Almost party time. All that hard work and sleepless nights and worry and gut-cramping stress and paranoia will be worth it. Because you and the girls will soon be living it up at Morven's family villa in Marbs. But that ain't all, folks. 'Cause Marbs is the literal warm-up, and glow-up (gotta love that Scottish-thistle complexion) to the most epic part of the summer holidays: a week of pre-season training in Portugal with the hockey squad and – wait for it, bear with me, drum roll please, no, really, this is the best bit – the rugby squad! A whole week of training, and chilling, on white sandy beaches, in the balmy heat of the Algarve, with the rugby boys. Hanging with, and getting to know, the sophisticated, experienced Upper Six girls. Partying with the Lower and Upper Six guys. Without parents. The holiday to end all holidays. The holiday of a lifetime. Forever known as That Summer. That Epic Summer!

But then you collapse. After your French written GCSE. You remember thinking, I'm going to puke, and then a stabbing pain in your stomach makes you double over and you don't remember anything else. Turns out your large intestine ruptured. When they got you to hospital and they looked inside you they discovered it was in shreds, all ulcered and perforated. They diagnosed ulcerative colitis and whipped out your dead colon there and then and gave you an ileostomy. Which basically means they brought the end of your remaining gut – your small intestine – to the surface of your tummy, stitched it there, slapped a sticky base-station thing – a flange – (don't expect me to use that word ever again) – around the hole – aka the stoma – and attached a bag on the top and that's how you poo right now. Into a bag. What every girl dreams of!

So here I am. In hospital. While everyone's getting wrecked at our end-of-term ball, celebrating the end of our GCSEs. Sorry, *their* GCSEs. I still had three exams left. I don't know when I'm supposed to do them. To catch up.

I don't really know anything right now. I really wish I hadn't given Julie those cans of Diet Coke . . .

I'm narky now. Like I want to smash up a few things. I'm just really, really fucking pissed off. I'm lying here at three in the morning looking at everyone's photos from tonight. Lockie, Meathead and Shawsie are in Morven's swimming pool at her after-party. That was our plan. Go back to hers, party until we couldn't stand, have a fry-up at crazy o'clock and crash out on the dining-room floor in our sleeping bags. I'm supposed to be there. I zoom in on a picture of Suriya, perched on the side of the pool laughing, in a new white bikini with gold medallion bits at the sides of the bottoms and at the tops of the triangles. And ponder her perfect belly for a moment.

I thought Morven would at least disinvite Lockie and Meathead after the Shit Bag thing . . . And Suriya said she'd give Lockie a piece of her mind!

He doesn't look particularly chastised. Almost naked in the pool . . . I can see he's lost muscle. I know the feeling. He's probably not been training over the last few weeks – partying, I guess. He looks good though. He's got some sun—

Dick! He's a total dick! I can't believe everyone's calling me Shit Bag now because of him. Who does that? What kind of squint-dicked, arachnophobic, Fruit Shoot-guzzling, Lego Friends master builder ex-boyfriend does that?

Lochlan Hamish Fingall Milling, that's who!

I mean, even if he did see my shit through the clear bag when I was off my face on morphine in High Dependency . . .

No! That was a test. And he's failed. Because any decent person wouldn't care and would love me for who I am. Not be totally obsessed with perfect boobs and pecs . . . and unscarred bellies!

In fact . . . Lockie Milling? Who is Lockie Milling? I haven't heard of him. Have I got any friends in my phone of that name? Nope. In any of my apps . . . ? Forgot that one. *Delete*. Nope, not even that app. No, I certainly do not have a single contact, ANYWHERE, with the name Lockie Milling. Thank God I don't know a guy called Lockie Milling. And I'll throw another thanks out there to the universe for the fact that I won't be able to see a hot blond guy called Lockie Milling in Meathead and Shawsie's photos either because – *Delete*. *Delete*.

CHAPTER 4

'I told you. I go by Shit Bag now. Only address me as Shit Bag.'

'You're a shitbag, alright,' Mum mutters under her breath, setting a can of Diet Coke on the kitchen table in front of Morven and another before me.

Is she actually joking? What kind of harpy taunts her daughter by flaunting a can of sweet-tasting explosive gas under her nose? After the Diet Coke wind incident in hospital a month ago, I haven't risked fizzy drinks. I don't have the back-up of a nurse to help me here if it all blows up. I snap, 'I can't drink that!'

Mum grabs the can and smacks it onto the kitchen island with a clunk. Essentially turning it into a fizz grenade. Then proceeds to slam cupboard doors for effect.

Morven's chewing the end of her thumbnail. She has a normal relationship with her parents, so she doesn't get the way we are. Hell, her parents *are* normal. Actually, my dad's normal. My mum, not so much.

Mum splashes a glass of Ribena onto the table and flounces out into the utility room. A few seconds later the back door slams. I curl my lip at the Ribena and fixate on the can of Diet Coke. If it's already agitated then I could just crack it open – it'll inevitably spray the counter and cabinets but Mum deserves that – and surely it'll be flat by the time I've decanted it into a glass and drunk it?

'I wish you could come with us to Portugal. Are you sure you can't?' Morven bites her bottom lip. 'You're starting to look more like . . . you.'

'Yesterday an old man in the GP's waiting room asked me if I had "the anorexia".'

'Yeah, but you're starting to look more *you* than you did in hospital. The sun might help?'

No amount of sun's going to feed my body back to match fitness. I'm not a houseplant. 'Stop rubbing it in, Morv. I can't play hockey right now! End of. Anyway, it's not like I can wear a bikini with this!' I point to my stomach.

'Well, you could . . .' Morven says. 'Remember that girl who posted the pic in her bikini showing her bag and—'

'No! I'm getting rid. Give me a couple of months and I'll be back to normal.'

'A couple! Really? I thought that chat group said it takes longer to heal?'

'*Usually*. But . . . mine'll be gone soon.' Even if I have to sew the damn thing up myself. YouTube'll have an instruction video . . .

'That's amazing, Frey!' She hugs me, and for once she's not dripping pity all over me.

I add for good measure, 'I'm gonna get a tattoo all the way down my stomach to cover my scars too. Then I can wear bikinis on the next hockey trip.'

'That'll be cool. I'd love a tattoo. What're you going to get? Wait, I thought you couldn't get a tattoo till you're eighteen? Maybe it's different if it's for medical reasons.'

'Your tan looks good,' I say, changing the subject and fiddling with my new silver friendship bracelet, a consolation present from Morven and her parents for missing the Marbella trip. 'Thanks for this.'

'Glad I got the small . . . Has Suriya been to see you yet?'

'No – haven't seen her since the end of term. What's with all her family gigs?'

'She promised she'd come see you before we leave for Portugal,' Morven says, shaking her head slightly.

'She told *me* she wouldn't make it before— It's fine. We'll video-call.'

Morven relayed the fight Suriya and Lockie had had at the ball. That Suriya reduced him to tears. Pretty impressive. I'm glad she's on my side. It would've been nice to know what Lockie actually said. But any time Suriya and me call, she just waves her hand and says, 'Who wants to waste time talking about him.'

Between you and me, I do. I'd really like to talk about Lockie. I know I told you he's dead to me, but over the last three-weeks-plus since I got out of hospital, I've felt like they forgot to inform me that they cut out part of my heart along with my gut.

'Have you seen him?' I say.

Morven purses her pale lips and nods.

'When?'

'A couple of times. His parents had a barbecue . . .'

WOAH! What? His parents had a barbecue? And they didn't invite us? I know I told Mum and Dad that I never wanted to speak to Lockie ever again, that if he visited they weren't to let him in, but, *obviously* if his parents invited us round then it would be social suicide and incredibly rude to say no! *That* would be the exception to the rule. Along with him being allowed to speak at my funeral to tell everyone how flipping great I am and how he'll never love anyone the way he loves (note the present tense) me!

We must've been invited – our mums are best mates, for fuck's sake – and Mum, the total cow, must've said, 'Ems, we'd love to, but Freya doesn't want to see Lockie.' Why the hell don't I have a normal mother?

I don't say any of this to Morven. I straighten my new bracelet and say, 'Is he well?'

She tips her head to the side as she shrugs. 'He's Lockie.'

Course he is.

We talk about Marbella some more and a little bit about Portugal. They're leaving in six days. She hasn't packed. Morven travels all over with her parents so it's not such a big deal for her. Me on the other hand, I started planning my outfit list over Easter. I found the page in my notebook last night. I did a ceremonial burning of it on my windowsill and let the ash float out into the cool night air. The birds were still singing. It was a nice ceremony. As for missing hockey, I was tempted to do a ceremonial bonfire with my sticks and kit bag to symbolise my sporting career ending. A pyre of ire. But I was too tired to trek downstairs and to the bottom of the garden, so I just chucked my sticks out the window into a bush. They're probably still there.

Seeing Morven – hugging Morven – that's been nice as well. So much more than nice! Amazing. Physical contact with the outside world. The *real* world. A crumb of teenage life – dropped into my starved, outstretched fingers.

But, worse, knowing that I'd had the chance to see Lockie. And Mum sabotaged that. Instead of being bundled up safe in one of his massive bearhugs. I was here, alone. That's reawakened the psychotic puppeteer and he's yanking at all the nerves in my belly. Not nice.

The doorbell chimes just as Morven's making noises about having to get away home. So we go to the door together.

'Beverley . . .' I say, surprised by this unscheduled visit from my district stoma nurse.

She's all smiles and gentleness. I both love and hate her for it. 'I was just passing by and thought – why don't I just pop in and see if Freya wants to have a go at changing her own ileostomy bag?'

Really hate her right now, actually. 'No. It's not a good time. I have a friend here.' Way to drag me back screaming and kicking to my new normal of hospitals and surgery and nurses and shit, Beverley!

'Oh, I'm just leaving.' Morven hugs me again before I can make eyes at her to stay. 'I'll message you later. Bye!' She waves brightly to Beverley and slips out the door, escaping my grim reality.

'Great!' Beverley says, rubbing her hands. 'Shall we do this together then?'

CHAPTER 5

'How did it go?' Mum says to Beverley, forty minutes later.

Beverley looks to me for an answer.

'Great,' I say.

'Well . . .' Beverley falters.

Traitor. I spin on my sock and skid across the hall's floorboards into the sitting room, slamming the door behind me. I wait for a bit and then realise that I'm not fooling anyone, so I grab the remote from the sofa and put on the TV. Then I creep back to the door to listen.

'Tell me she changed it herself?'

'Unfortunately not. She says she doesn't have to learn because *it's temporary . . .*'

Mum shrieks, 'It'll be at least five months before they reverse it. I can't keep—'

Here we go. Bring on the waterworks. Just like you do with Dad.

'Shhh, it's okay. I have an idea.' Beverley engages a soothing tone as she moves past the sitting-room. 'A way to help her deal with it. And take some pressure off you.'

I lean in closer to the door.

'Really?' Mum snivels, her voice heading for the kitchen. 'I'm sorry I'm being like this, but I want to faint every time I look at it.'

'Okay . . . well, I expect Freya feels something similar . . .'

What? I don't feel like fainting! I'm not similar to *her*! I just don't . . . You would understand if you'd seen *it*. The bags are opaque now, a pinky-beige colour. So I can't see the *stoma* inside. You know, that bit of gut lining they brought to the surface of my tummy.

But I can't shrug that first sighting – back in the hospital – from my head.

They use clear poo bags at the start so, according to the fit student doctor with the big hands, they can see inside, in case the bag starts filling with blood instead of the 'normal' green-bile-tinted poo. Or if the stoma becomes twisted, cut off from the blood supply, turns black and falls off or something. Great chat-up conversations Big Hands and me had. Real turn-on!

But that's my point, they didn't warn me. About that extra shock. They just left me with the clear plastic bag so that when I was alone on the ward, I unsuspectingly took a little look and there it was inside. The stoma. The opening. Like a sea anemone without tentacles. Red. Alien. The *ultimate* rude body part. Something too dirty for anyone to see, even my own eyes.

And there lies my issue. At first, I thought Lockie ghosted me because he'd seen my poo inside the bag. But what if he saw my stoma too? How can I ever look him in the eye again? How can we ever be normal together? After he's actually seen my guts.

My life as I knew it is over.

So why shouldn't Mum be the one to look at that gaping red hole as she unpeels the old bag? Ungluing the sticky base from my slashed tummy with clinical alcohol, ripping every teeny, tiny hair off with it, stinging and nipping at any raw sore. Why shouldn't she do whatever else it is she has to do – while I'm enduring all the pain and staring at the dead fly caught in the cobweb in the corner of the bathroom – before she sticks on the brand-new unsullied bag? She's my mother. I'm the child. I shouldn't have to go through this on my own.

Hell! I'm emptying the shitting thing. What more do they want from me?

A lot, it turns out, because instead of living it up in Portugal for the rest of my summer holidays or lying on a garden lounger and binge-streaming movies and TV with Winston and Nibblet for company, I'm being dragged to the ninth circle of hell by my traitorous parents. More commonly known as outward-bound camp. Outward Bound! Thank you, Beverley, *great* idea.

Picture this for a scenario. A load of strangers – well, families who don't know each other – spend a week together at an outward-bound camp on the side of a loch in the Highlands of Scotland. Sounds not *that* bad? No? Sure? Well, imagine if at least one of the kids in each family has a problem with their bowel. They've either – according to Beverley and her questionable sales pitch – had it removed, or it's falling apart and soon to be removed, or they've had a surgeon hack it to bits and sew it back together or they've got a bag like me.

Some bright spark thought, where's the best place to put a load of kids with bowel continence issues?

I know! Let's dump them in the middle of a forest. Somewhere with just a couple of communal bogs, at the far, far end of a midge-infested loch. And then let's push their bodies to the limits in the wild Highlands of Scotland – canoeing, orienteering, raft-building, climbing mountains, jumping in freezing lochs. Despite the fact most of those kids are (Beverley was really selling it at this stage) bony and scrawny – just like you, Freya! – because they've been through physical trauma and near starvation while their

29

guts have been *killing them* instead of absorbing vital nutrients so they can live their best lives.

What a bloody great idea! Let's have our annual get-together for this inflammatory bowel disease charity at a wild outward-bound camp near Callander.

Why, yes, let's!

CHAPTER 6

'We need to leave now, Freya. Freya!'

'What, Mum?'

'I said, we're leaving now.'

'Bye then.'

'Get up off the bean bag.'

I grit my teeth.

'Up!'

'Make me.'

'Fine.'

'Oww! Let go. Oww, you're hurting me. Dad! Daad!'

'He's outside in the car. Waiting!'

'You're hurting my scar. You'll burst my stitches!'

'Then walk properly and you won't burst them.'

Mum hustles me down the stairs and out the front door into the back of the car. I fold my arms and mutter, 'This is child abuse.'

Mum sets the house alarm and locks the front door. She gets in and buckles up.

'My satchel's upstairs.'

'What?'

'I said, my bag's in my room.'

'Why didn't you bring it?' Dad says to Mum.

'Why didn't *I* bring it?'

'Yeah, Mum, why didn't *you* bring it?'

'I swear to God . . .' Mum hisses. She slams the car door, and then the porch door against the wall and leaves the alarm first beeping and then wailing. She finally emerges five minutes later with my satchel and the rucksack she told me 'not to forget'. She shoves the rucksack in the boot then, back in the car, throws my bag at me and puts something else in the glove compartment. 'We're going to be late now,' she seethes.

I twitch my nose as Dad reverses. Finally recognising the acrid tang, I say, 'I can smell smoke.'

Dad pauses, arms and shoulders contorted in his manoeuvres. 'Did you just have a cigarette?'

Mum snaps round, red-faced, like she's going to punch him, and says, 'Yes . . . I fucking did . . .'

So as you can see, my mum's holding on to the last remnant of her sanity by a single, fraying thread. Apparently growing up in a family of five siblings – I have enough aunties, uncles and cousins to field a football match – was way easier for her to deal with than living with me. And Dad.

We brew in silence for most of the journey. Mum stands in the car park at Stirling Services, after I've been to empty my bag in the disabled loo, and smokes a Marlboro Gold. She glares defiantly down her nose at me when she exhales the plume of smoke into the air. I guess that last thread has finally snapped.

I sift through pictures in my apps of the hockey and rugby squads at Edinburgh airport, from their plane journey and then on the coach from Faro. Looking for Lockie.

I wake realising that the car has stopped moving. I'm alone. For once they *don't* wake me and it's to leave me sleeping in a public car park. Exemplary parenting.

Bark chip on the ground, felled tree trunks propped on logs around the boundary. Rustic. We're here then. I lean forward between the front seats to see the murky loch with its pebble shore. All around, on the horizon and behind me – God! Twisting. It gets me in the gut every time I do it – are towering pines with bare trunks and bristly green caps. Like a company of ancient bog brushes ready to go to war on the giant toilet bowl of the loch.

It's five thirty. I'm hungry. And thirsty – I take a gulp

from my water bottle. Each of my apps says 'No Internet Connection. Use Wi-Fi to Access Data' etc. The last image I was looking at before I fell asleep was a selfie taken by our goalie. Over her shoulder, I can see Lockie leaning on the headrest, two seats behind. He's wearing a loose acid-pink vest and mirrored aviators. I screenshot it just in case it's the last picture I can access, and try to phone Mum. The phone beeps, protesting that there's no reception. I really am in the ninth circle of hell.

Mum appears ten minutes later. 'Are you getting out?'

'Have they got Wi-Fi here?'

'I don't know, Freya, probably.' She holds my door open. I climb down, put my satchel on my shoulder. Mum shuts my door and locks the car.

'What about our bags?'

'We unpacked when you were sleeping.'

I fold my arms and screw up my lips. 'Yeah, nice of you to leave me alone . . . Where's Dad?'

'Inside.'

I trail behind her past a log cabin with a rainbow of canoes stacked on racks. Past a picnic area with brick barbecues and tables, and an open-sided metal shed with sinks and draining boards. She starts up a snaking brick path. 'How much further?' I huff.

'There.'

At the top of the hill, tucked into the trees as if for

shelter, is a two-storey granite hunting lodge. Running off to its left and right, like arms extending and bending at the elbows, are long stone-and-wood bothies. I hunch over, giving in to the tugging of my scar and the need to fill my lungs. Just a wee breather, then I'm ready for an Ironman. Delusional, much.

Once we make it inside the main building, I discover a sparse mix between hunting lodge, army barracks and hostel. To the right, Mum pushes through a fire door with wire mesh in the glass and we join a rubber-floored corridor. I guess we're in one of the arm extensions. On either side are doors, all numbered, and the only natural light beyond the glare of the strip lights comes from Veluxes in the pitched roof. I follow Mum into cell number ten. Two single beds. Dad lying with his feet up on the one by the door, watching football on his phone. One wardrobe. Two chests of drawers. Surprisingly no bars on the door or slide-bolts on the outside. 'We're not sharing a room, are we? How are you both going to sleep on that?' I sit on the bed nearest the window and try my phone again. 'Drop me the Wi-Fi password, will you, Dad.' I hear a wet sound like when I chew gum angrily and look up – Mum and Dad are mouthing at each other and waving their arms. 'What?' I say.

'I thought your mum told you.'

'Told me what?'

'Why should I have to tell her? You could've told her. Anyway, she wouldn't have agreed if I had.'

'Agreed to what?'

Dad flounders. 'Well . . . you're . . .'

I narrow my eyes. Take in the luggage on the floor. 'Where's your stuff?'

Mum sighs and rolls her eyes. 'We're not staying.'

'What do you mean, you're not staying?'

'They said it'll help you integrate. Peer support.'

'They? Who the hell're *they*?'

There's a crowd roar from Dad's phone and he gasps with exasperation that he just missed a goal. Apparently football's more important than his only child.

'It doesn't matter,' Mum says. 'Less of the swearing while you're here.'

Right, Mum, because I'm going to listen to you, now you're abandoning me.

'You'll meet other kids with the same issues. Learn how to deal with your bag,' she says, as if she's reading from a holiday brochure.

'Oh. Okay! You're dumping me here to *deal* with my issues. Maybe you're the one who can't deal with my *issues*! How long?'

'Six nights.'

'Six! I can't believe— What if I have to change my bag?' Panic boils up inside me. I'm in serious danger of crying.

36

'I'm not – I'm not doing it!' I put my hands over my face and suck air in through my nostrils. I feel my stoma move and my bag feels hot against my belly. 'GAHHHHH!' I scream, and find myself standing. 'I FUCKING HATE YOU!' My whole body is in flames. I thump past Mum and Dad, swing open the cell door and just manage to avoid smacking into a tall girl who's clearly been eavesdropping in the hall. 'Do you think you could get out of my way—!' I seethe at her. She moves, but she's all wide-eyed and raised brows, judging me.

'Freya!' Mum says behind me.

I swing round, snarling at Mum but manage for once not to scream 'FUCK OFF' because we're being watched like zoo animals by Miss Judgy Long Legs and, instead, shove the door back into the room with such force that it smacks against the door-stop and makes a cracking sound. Show's over. I ignore the gawking girl when she stands back against the wall in the narrow corridor, arms raised in surrender like I'm going to hit her or some shit like that. And I manage to walk away without my legs collapsing, to thankfully find what I'm looking for – a door with a symbol of a bod in a dress. Nice. Inclusive.

CHAPTER 7

Heart thumping out of my chest, I find a stark row of sinks, showers and loo cubicles. I pee first, then, with shaking fingers, I empty my bag, wipe the opening with tissue, reclip and flush. I'll just have to go the whole six nights with the same flange and bag. There, I've said it again. Flange. Flange, flange, flange, flange, FLANGE! It sounds so much worse than adhesive base station, but right now flange is exactly how I feel. FLANGE! They can't bully me into this. This isn't part of the plan. Mum's supposed to change my bag over the next four, maybe five, months – then, when I'm stronger, the surgeon will make me a man-made (woman-made?) reservoir out of my small intestine, called a pouch. An internal gut-bag sort of thing. It won't work totally like my old colon – that tattered bit of exploding gut they chucked in the bin – but as far as I'm concerned, a pouch on the inside is so much better than carrying a poo bag on the *outside*.

And when I get rid of this poo bag – I'll get rid of Shit Bag! Lockie won't be disgusted by me anymore, Suriya won't be acting like she doesn't have time in her busy schedule to fit me in, and Morven will stop treating me like a charity case. I'll bulk up again, get my fitness back and take my place in the hockey squad. *Everything* will just go back to how it used to be!

THAT is the plan.

The thought of changing my bag, looking under there . . . it makes me feel sick. And all that skin ripping and nipping and stinging! And what if the stoma poos while I'm doing it and I actually *do* faint? Or puke? Or I puke and faint? And where's the table to lay out all the stuff like the bathroom at home? What's everyone else here going to do? There must be others with bags. What about that girl? Maybe she's got one. *She* could do it for me. If I hadn't just screamed in her face and made her instantly hate me.

I'm at the hand-dryer.

A girl with bleached hair, a moon-face and bad extensions flies through the door and into one of the cubicles.

And so the freak show begins.

My hands are almost dry. I hit the button again and get out quick. One thing I've realised over the last few months.

No one wants stragglers hanging around at the mirror checking their make-up when you're on the loo. Even when you're normal, you want privacy. And that's the point. No one's normal here. Me included.

Outside, I lean against the wall and breathe. I check my phone. Nothing. I make for the reception in the main building and find the Wi-Fi password inside a plastic frame on the desk.

Now what? I'm not going back to that room. Mum and Dad can sweat it out with Miss Judgy Face for a while. She's bound to piss Mum off – Mum hates feeling criticised. So maybe when I *do* go back, they'll have repacked the car and be ready to take me home, away from this toxic environment. I walk outside, keeping an eye on the Wi-Fi signal on my phone, turning right so Mum and Dad can't see me from that tiny prison cell they're planning on leaving me in.

I mean, what's actually wrong with them?

At the end of the extension block there are steps down the hill to a kids' play area with swings and a huge caber log at an angle with a giant, dish-shaped spiderweb hanging from it. I want to get into the rope spiderweb. I want to lie in there and swing back and forth until I get so dizzy, I pass out. But I suspect, just like a fly, I'll get stuck because my bloody stomach muscles are flanged! I'm *flanged*.

I sit on one of the swings. Damn it. I left my water bottle

in the prison cell. I'm parched. I should've looked for a water fountain. That's the problem with not having a colon – dehydration. Apparently, I lose thirty percent more water than normal people. I flick to another picture on my phone showing Lockie, Meathead, Shawsie and a couple of other rugby guys from my year sunning themselves on the patio of a whitewashed bungalow. They're all topless, in their shorts with their feet propped up on a low wall. Sweaty. I guess the heat of Portugal wouldn't have been the best idea for me right now – not while I've got *this*.

Two little kids run down the slope and freeze when they see me, as if I'm dangerous.

'It's okay, come and swing if you want,' I say.

The girl struts forward and plonks herself onto the seat by me. The boy's not so bold and hangs back with his thumb in his mouth, practically rubbing up against a bush like a cat.

'I'm Jessica.' She juts out her hand.

I recoil before realising I'm supposed to shake it. 'Freya,' I say.

'That's Henry. We just met.'

'Henry!' I lift my head at him.

'Henry's got an ostomy too,' she says, as she kicks off with one leg and hitches herself onto the middle of the swing's seat.

What? They're only babies! 'Do you have a bag, Jessica?'

Jessica nods enthusiastically. 'Do you want to see it? It's got Batman today.'

'Batman?'

Jessica stops swinging and pulls up her little T-shirt. I guess she must be about five . . . surely not six? I can't get my head round this. Her parents can't leave her here alone! She proudly pushes her tummy towards me, showing off her bag. It's smaller and doesn't have the drainage hole at the bottom like mine so I guess hers is a colostomy bag. So, unlike me, she still has some of her colon left. I'm glad for her that she won't have to empty her bag quite as often as me. That her body still absorbs the water it should and her poo is more . . . firm. Sorry. TMI. Anyway, someone, a parent probably, has taped all over the bag with Batman duct tape so that the whole surface is covered in winged logos. A clever way to camouflage the whole utilitarian, medical apparatus vibe. If only I'd been rocking some Caped Crusader tape over that clear bag in High Dependency.

'Nice bag, Jessica!'

'I have Superman and Wonder Woman and Thor and Iron Man. My daddy makes them for me.'

By now Henry has joined us and he's staring at Jessica's bag in awe.

'What about you, Henners?' Granny had a cat called Henry. We called him Henners. 'Tell me you're repping Sersi, Ms Marvel, Echo, Loki and Ironheart?'

He flinches into himself like a tortoise and shakes his head.

'Where's your daddy, Jessica? Do you think he's got more tape we could use?'

She shakes her head. 'He's in the canteen up there but he keeps it in the garage at home.'

'Hmm. I wonder where I can get some to decorate my bag?' I say, pulling up my vest top to show them my boring beige poo bag.

Both their mouths fall open, surprised to see that I'm part of their club too. Henry recovers quickest. 'Please can you decorate mine too?' He pulls his T-shirt up and sticks his tummy out proudly.

'Definitely,' I say. Shit. Does this mean I have to stay now? Are these little kids a plant to make me stay? I look back towards the lodge. Is this one big social experiment orchestrated by some evil-genius stoma nurse? Is Beverley in there somewhere, watching me right now on camera . . . ?

CHAPTER 8

Leaving my little buddies playing, I conceded defeat about fifteen minutes ago and came back to my cell to get my water bottle. Thankfully Miss Judgy Long Legs is nowhere to be seen. Though there is a big canvas travel bag sitting on the other bed. I'm pretty tired with all the drama so I'm lying on the torture device masquerading as my bed, zoned out, looking through friends' social media. Least the Wi-Fi signal in this penitentiary reaches the cells.

A message from Mum flashes up. I flick it out of the way without reading it. I'm deep in stalking mode when another message appears.

> **Mum:** Where are you? The induction has already started. Get here now, Freya!

I look at her previous message.

Mum: The stoma nurse is doing an induction talk in five minutes. You need to come to the common room behind reception. They're doing an icebreaker straight after for all the teens. Come now.

I tug self-consciously at the bottom of my vest top, all too aware of my bag underneath it. What if I'm the only teen here who has a bag? Maybe it's just me, Henners and Jessica with bags, and everyone else is *avec* mildly dysfunctional large and small bowels . . .

And even if there are others, I don't want them to know just by looking at me.

Like Miss Judgy Long Legs over there with the big canvas bag. If that's the only bag she brought with her, then there's no way I want her to know I have a poo bag.

Or maybe I do the opposite! Mix it up. And just show them my bag. Let it hang out the bottom of my vest top, like that girl Morven and me saw on Insta with her bag all flapping around loose when she was in her bikini. What? This little thing? Yeah, it's this season – Spring/Summer . . . Maybe do a catwalk and stick my belly out like little Jessica. I might like it. Enjoy the air circulating. It'll be less sweaty in this weather.

Yeah! Not a chance. Not. A. Chance, in this ninth circle of hell am I flashing a group of randos my shit-carrier bag!

I pull on my hoodie and zip it up to cover the tell-tale circle outline showing through my vest, like the ring from those horror films *The Ring* and *Rings*. That's how the bag clips onto the flange. FLANGE! With the ring.

You're probably wondering how I know it connects like that considering I refuse to look below the surface. Well, Beverley, my double-crossing stoma nurse, forced me to at least examine the apparatus, I just haven't done it *in situ*. What do I care how it snaps together and the clip works and how it all covers this mysterious, evil thing called a stoma? Well, apparently, Beverley pointed out, *I should care*, because what happens if it leaks or falls off when Mum isn't around? What do I do then?

Good bloody question!

Perhaps I will go meet that stoma nurse at the induction. Because someone's going to have to change my bag while I'm here. And it ain't gonna be me.

But first, I need to revisit my favourite hang-out spot and empty my bag again.

I push in through double swing doors into a large room with white walls and bright-blue carpet tiles, and realise immediately that I've messed up. A bunch of teenagers sitting in a circle of chairs, maybe a dozen or so, stare at me.

'I'm looking for the induction talk?'

'You missed it,' a girl says.

I scan the circle, looking for the owner of the voice. And recognise her judgy eyebrows first.

'They've gone to the canteen,' my roommate says.

'Oh, okay . . .' I reach to pull the door handle.

'So you're not joining in? We're supposed to be doing the icebreaker now.'

'Uh, well, I . . .' They're still staring. All of them. Bollocks! 'Alright . . .' I move into the room and some of the kids at least have the decency to look back to the circle again. A tall boy in a navy Merchants School tracksuit – a fellow Edinburgh school, small world – with brown skin and close-cropped dark hair gets up and grabs another chair for me. And he and his neighbour budge apart to make room. Suddenly I'm sitting between them and I'm part of the group. I clamp my arms across my front and avoid eye contact with the girl opposite me, just to be clear I'm not letting anyone in. Try and break my ice? Not a chance. I'm frozen solid.

'We're introducing ourselves,' my roommate says. 'Name, age, where you're from, what your health condition is – if you're comfortable sharing that info – how long you've had it. Stuff like that.'

I nod imperceptibly.

'Carry on, Cody,' Roommate says.

I look out of the corner of my eye at Cody. It's the girl with the full-moon face who ran into the loo earlier. 'So, I'm Cody,' she says. 'I'm from Livingston. I'm fifteen.' Fifteen? She looks twelve tops. 'I have Crohn's disease. My face is fat because I'm on steroids right now.' There's a rumble of supportive protest around the circle and I feel bad that my immediate thought was – oh, *that's why her face is round*. I offer up a reassuring smile when she catches my eye. 'And I've had Crohn's since I was eight,' she finishes. Yikes. That's brutal. It suddenly occurs to me that I don't know much about Crohn's, or ulcerative colitis, or steroids, or any of this.

Next is the boy to my right.

'Owen.'

I venture a neck-crank and take in his K-pop idol hair and oversized skater clothes. His arms are crossed at the waist. We're all about open body language on this side of the circle.

'I'm fourteen,' he says. 'I live in Stirling but I'm originally from Neath in Wales, and I have Crohn's, like Cody.'

He smiles at Cody and I take the opportunity to look around the circle. To gauge the ages of the other group members. He continues, 'I was only diagnosed a year and a half ago. I'm between flares at the moment.'

Everyone round the circle nods and seems pleased about this. Like it's a good thing. If Owen and Cody are only a year or two younger than me, then perhaps the pre-teen lookalikes are closer to my age than I thought.

Silence settles around the circle. My roommate says, 'Can you tell us about yourself, Freya?'

And I don't know why this sets me off but the fact this girl, *who doesn't know me at all*, knows my name and I don't know hers. Like she's got something over me already. I'm triggered.

So I open my mouth and let it flow. 'Sure,' I say. 'My name's Shit Bag . . .'

Someone gasps.

Roommate protests, 'Excuse me!'

I talk over her. 'I'm from Edinburgh. By pure coincidence, I've got a bag of shit stuck to my stomach so it's lucky my parents had the foresight to name me Shit Bag.' There's a snigger to my left. 'I got rushed to hospital about seven weeks ago. They said something about ulcerative colitis but that seems irrelevant considering they'd already cut out my colon. Um, my mum wants to faint when she looks at my stoma. And . . . I'm sixteen!'

The boy in the Merchants tracksuit to my left whistles and when I look, I see he's laughing. One of those open-mouthed laughs you do when you can't believe someone's said something that outrageous. Yep, my work here is done.

Perhaps whoever's watching us like lab rats will decide I'm too much of a disruptive force to stay and they'll help Mum and Dad repack the car.

'Your turn,' I say, saccharin-sweet to the boy next to me, who's still laughing. He has the most vivid blue-green eyes. Who are you? What year are you in? What's your sport of choice to go with that tracksuit? Tell me more about the only person in the room who appreciates my kind of sarcasm.

He says, 'How do I follow that?'

'By not being really offensive,' Roommate chimes in. 'Show some respect!'

'She's fine, Mel,' Merchants Tracksuit Boy says, waving for her to calm down. 'It's kind of funny.'

Yeah, Mel. I'm fine. And kind of funny . . . I wait for the Blue-Green-Eyed Tracksuit Boy to tell us all about himself.

'No, Chris!' Mel interrupts again, getting a bit ranty. *Ah, so he's called Chris . . .* 'She completely missed what Mum said at induction – she's definitely not thinking of the other people here with ostomies. Or the people considering getting one. That's the whole point of this camp, *Freya*. Moral support. Respecting one another. Building up our confidence. Pushing ourselves out of our comfort zones in a *safe* environment. You're not making this safe, Freya.'

My heart's thundering. I'm kind of mortified. And at the same time I want to tell this girl – Mel – to go draw her pension. How old is she? She sounds like a teacher. But I don't say anything. Instead, I yawn. A massive (no understatement) – MASSIVE – yawn.

And Chris spits air, laughing again.

What? I'm tired! It's been a long day.

'Is this one big joke to you?' Mel killjoys.

You know when you start yawning. You just can't stop sometimes. Yeah, well, they're like buses. Coming all at once.

Mel says, 'I think you've had enough airtime, Freya. Introduce yourself, Chris.'

Chris turns to look at me and quirks his lips. 'My name's Chris.' He flicks his eyebrows briefly, confidently. 'I'm seventeen,' he says to me. 'I live local, Perthshire, but I'm at boarding school in Edinburgh.'

And he looks away to the others but that quirk at the side of his mouth lingers on my side for a moment like he's reluctant to turn serious. Then he says, 'I've got Crohn's too, had it for seven years. Me and Mel met at an IBD social way back. We've been through it together, haven't we, Melly?' He reaches his hand out to my roommate and touches her arm. She gives him this knowing smile. 'Mel's better informed than the rest of us,' he continues. 'Seeing as her mum's the stoma nurse who set this whole camp up.' *Aw, shit!* I heard her mention 'Mum' but I didn't connect. And then he says, as if he'd forgotten, 'Oh yeah, and I've had my shit bag for just over six months.'

Oh!

I turn to check he's being legit. Witness a flash of his dimpled grin towards Mel.

And barely a flicker on *her* poker face. She says, 'My name's Mel,' all businesslike. 'I'm seventeen. From Glasgow. I was diagnosed with ulcerative colitis at seven, so I've had it a long time. Two years ago, I had a flare that didn't respond to medication and so I opted for a complete colectomy and pouch formation. Which means they removed my large intestine. I had an ileostomy for a little while so things could heal. Then they did a reversal. And now, for the last year, I've lived with an ileoanal pouch – also known as a J-pouch. Named after the shape they make when they sew two lengths of small intestine into a J-shaped pouch that stands in for my removed colon. Historically there were other pouch designs – W, S, K pouches (Ks are a bit different) but J-pouches are what they tend to go with now. Anyway, yeah, as Chris said, that was my mum at the induction. She set up this camp because she works with ostomates every day and we've lived my IBD journey as a family for a decade. Our daily activities at camp have been designed with those experiences in mind – to boost our confidence not just physically but psychologically too.'

I want to interrupt her with a snide *'Psychologically? So we are lab rats!'* But all I'm focused on in Mel's biology and history textbook lecture is . . . *she has a pouch*! The very thing I want. The answer to me getting rid of this bag of shit on my stomach.

I've just managed to piss off the one person here who can really tell me what my life will be like after I get rid of my bag. This girl holds the knowledge on my future. And clearly she now hates me. Way to go, Shit Bag!

CHAPTER 9

Mum and Dad have just driven away, leaving me.

At least they stayed for dinner, so I wasn't a total Norma Nae Mates. And Cody, the girl with the sweet round face, sat with us along with her parents. We had a nice chat. Turns out her mum and dad are staying for the entire camp, because that's possible (even mandatory for the little kids). Evidently, Cody's parents like her a whole lot more than mine do me. But I guess mine have their uses. They redeemed themselves, just a smidge, by introing me to the stoma nurse – Annabelle; Mel's mum – before they went. So at least the bag-change crisis has been averted.

As for the other *situation*, I need to broker some sort of peace with Mel, so she'll speak to me about her pouch.

She and Chris sat together for dinner, far enough away across the canteen that I could watch them unobserved.

There's definitely something going on there (or has gone on) – they're super into touching and hugging. That was Lockie and me, when things were good.

There's a movie on in the common room tonight but as I'm tired from today and I'm not sure where Cody is – I stupidly went to empty my bag and didn't ask her to wait for me – I go to my cell and lie on my hard bed. I'm back on the yawning train again. If Mel was here she might even believe my earlier yawns were genuine and I wasn't *just* being a dick. As for Chris, I can't believe he's got an ostomy. He doesn't look like he has one. I mean . . . What does someone look like who has an ostomy? Emaciated like me? He's not as bulky as Lockie. But he's taller. Most guys aren't quite as hench as Lockie when they're taller. Unless they're Meathead. But he's just a mountain of . . . meat. Rancid meat. That lump brings nothing palatable to the friendship table.

And suddenly I'm compulsively scanning Morven's then Suriya's socials, in search of a Lockie fix. Suriya obliges with a perfect, looking-at-the-camera-from-across-the-room photo of him between Meathead and a guy from the year above. They're in a pizza restaurant, going by the plates, and it's those straight-down-the-lens, piercing pale-blue eyes looking at me that hit me sensitive. They should probably creep me out. Like a spooky painting's eyes following you around the room. But I find them reassuring.

He's always been watching. Always has my back. Always comes to my rescue. And me his.

Only . . . This time. He hasn't.

Well, he did at the very start. He visited in the first few High Dependency days. Mum told me he'd insisted, even though only family were allowed. She lied to the hospital and told them he was my brother so he could come into the near-silent emergency recovery ward – silent bar the beeps and alarms and nurses talking in raised voices to reach the ears of their barely conscious patients. My memory's patchy. But I do remember that he was there. Even though reality was muffled by a plump duvet of morphine. And a car-crash trauma to my abdomen – strangely solid and numb, unbending – that I didn't understand. Hadn't yet witnessed the butchery under the white dressings. I remember him holding my hand though. He always holds my hand.

Always did.

The longer I lie here looking at photos and videos of Lockie, the darker my head slips. I keep replaying that second time Lockie came to hospital – with Ems and John, his mum and dad. I was awake by then and traumatised but still me. Still ready to chat and self-deprecate. Put on a brave face. Ready for him to hug me and kiss me and tell me he'd be there with me.

But yeah, it hasn't worked out like that. I guess you

don't know the people around you as well as you think you do.

Mel's probably staying out on purpose. Her luggage is still on her bed, so she can't have moved rooms. Would she do that? She could easily ask her mum. Who else would they put in with me? Cody would be okay. But what if Cody's gone to the common room and Mel turns her against me too?

I get ready for bed. I have to do things back to front because it's a communal bathroom. So I empty my bag and wash up and clean my teeth etc, all before I go back to my room and change into my pyjamas. I'm not sure how it will be when I have to use the loo through the night. What if the distance means I don't make it in time? What if my bag is so full and heavy that it rips off on the way there? Least Mum packed my dressing gown. Handy that – spending weeks in hospital – you have no trouble checking that swag item off the packing list. We're probably all strong on the granny and grandad aesthetic here, with our new, oddly presentable for public viewings, dressing gowns and slippers. Like a sick-kid uniform. I wonder what Chris wears . . .

Still with no sign of Mel, I put the light out and my AirPods in just before eleven p.m., and the next thing I know the light from the hall is spotlighting me through the dark. I barely register if the black silhouette is Mel as she slips outside and closes the door.

What time is it?

I reach for my phone and see it's almost three a.m. Ugh. This is like being on a hospital ward all over again. Getting woken through the night. I should've brought the noise-cancelling sleep mask Dad bought me, least it wouldn't wreck my eardrum when I lie on my left side. I pull the duvet higher over my head and push the one AirPod I can handle properly into my right ear. I try nodding my head into the pillow to try and block out my thoughts. To fight the urge to sit up and sweep through classmates' photos for a new image of Lockie. I'm regretting deleting him as a friend now. I can't even save the pictures he had of us together.

Great. Now all I want is to see him. To see everyone! To check in on what they're doing without me. It's like a compulsion. To look at the life I'm missing. My old life. The life I should be living right now.

I don't want to be here. This pillowcase smells of chemicals. And this mattress is so bloody hard! I reposition onto my back and immediately realise my bag's working the head-on-collision look – it's full of air.

So with the grace of an elephant seal, I roll back onto my left hip and lever myself up to sitting. You lot who haven't had your stomach muscles cut through – don't know how lucky you are. You take loads of things for granted. Sitting up in bed, for one. You probably don't realise it, but you use your stomach muscles for that. Then there's sneezing. Sneezing's fun. They say it's like a mini orgasm, don't they? Not for me now. These days sneezing's like what I imagine Noomi Rapace experienced in *Prometheus* when she had to cut the baby squid alien out of her. *If* she hadn't had that magic painkilling pen she jabbed herself with.

Anyway, I grab my phone and missing AirPod, and with my eyes screwed up against the light in the corridor, I get to the bathroom. Two of the cubicle doors are signalling red. Only at a camp like ours are teens having poo parties in the early hours. God we're flanged!

I shout, 'Just a bagger. Won't be long. But I've got noise-cancelling AirPods and my music up loud so don't be shy. Knock yourselves out!'

Just before I press play, I hear a voice – is it Mel's? – quietly say, 'Thanks.'

I remember what it was like before. Before my bag. Before they cut out my gut. Hell. Hell on earth. You're basically a cramping, butt-cheek clamping, gassy, shitting machine. Anything you eat or drink seems to do it. I mean, I'd eat a raspberry – well maybe four or five – and before they could even hit my stomach my guts had started to squeal like an angry cat being scrubbed in the kitchen sink, a sink with a leaking, glugging plughole. I'm not talking stomach acid getting ready to digest stuff, I mean way down below. I don't know . . . we didn't cover that phenomenon in GCSE biology.

How I didn't think to talk to someone about that! But I just thought it was a bit of IBS caused by exam stress.

I wipe a couple of little splashes under the rim with tissue and flush the loo. Wash my hands and make sure to give the dryer another punch on my way out.

Back in the room, I arrange a clean towel and a pair of trackies like bolster sausages on the bed around me, to take some pressure off my protruding hip and coccyx bones, turn the volume right down on my music and pull the duvet over my head to block out my immediate reality.

The more I think about it, I should be seriously happy that I'm a step closer to having a normal life again and getting my bag reversed, because the way things were before I got rushed to hospital . . . they were grim. There was blood! When I wiped. At first I crapped myself, metaphorically, thinking I had cancer or something. But then I read online that it could be piles – from sitting and revising too much. So I didn't say anything to anyone. Just tried to be more active . . . and avoid raspberries.

But it wasn't just raspberries.

And I was desperate for the loo all the time. Like run

fast off the hockey pitch at the end of the game or I'm really, really going to regret it. Even worse was the noise. That angry, strangulated cat noise is the sign of wind. And partner that with the stuff coming out. The rotting, dead animal paired with over-boiled cabbage, diarrhoea stench. Well, you can totally imagine. Yeah, okay, I probably went a bit too far on that previous detail but you're either in or you're out on this story. Come along with me on this foul, shitty ride or bail out now. It's your choice.

Hey, at least you have a choice.

There were even a couple of times, at school, when I hadn't realised someone else was in the loos and they heard me. *Mortifying*. But the worst was at Morven's sixteenth. Morven's parents are minted. She had her sixteenth party in a marquee with a black-tie dress code but a cowboy/cowgirl theme – her mum wanted the black tie and Morven wanted the cowboy/cowgirl. Morven had planned on wearing leather chaps and not much else – but in the end her mum found her this sequinned dress in cow print. Sounds trashy but actually it was fire. It was a sit-down dinner first. And in keeping with the theme, we had a Texan BBQ. With fried beans and, oh God, there was even sweetcorn. Sweetcorn is the enemy. There was a milkshake bar and a cow-print ice-cream van. I don't do well with dairy either.

After the food and lactose everyone else was dancing in the marquee having the time of their lives before doomsday started, aka our exams. Or they were outside with their tongue stuck down the throat of their partner in crime or a stranger.

Not me. I was in the posh Portaloos having a shit time. That feels so long ago now, like I'm a totally different person. I suppose I am, physically anyway. It's scary how much can change in a few months.

I strike another match. The blaze reflects my mood.

Another gut-wrenching spasm constricts. I cringe and shake out the flame so that my nostrils at least fill with the sweet sulphurous stench of smoke. I hear laughter over the thumping music. Girls. I close my eyes in pain. Go past. Please!

'Oh my God! It absolutely stinks in here.'

'Ugh! That's so gross.'

'There's someone still in there.'

'Shh!' Giggles. Gags. 'Okay in there?' the girl shouts.

Both snort and spit laughter.

'It's like something's died,' the other says. 'Come on, let's pee in the bushes. That's just wrong . . .'

Fifteen minutes and three more judgemental Portaloo visitors later, I stand and stare. The mirror's

Hollywood bulbs glare at my puffy face. We've been mixing Prosecco with Red Bull. I feel sick.

I dry my hands and chuck the paper towel. Unzip my micro shoulder bag and pull out stuff until I find the packet crammed in the bottom. I carry an arsenal in my tiny bag. Tissues — dry and moist. Matches. Pant liners. Atomiser-air-freshener. All that sort of stuff. I pop a couple more of my green-and-grey pills. Just two left. Turn the tap back on. This probably isn't drinking water. After I've swallowed, I wash my hands again and dry them. Trembling, I replait my cowgirl braids. Put on more lipstick. Hot pink. To contrast with my denim skater dress. I spray the perfume from the little basket by the sink all over me and into the cubicle. I pause for a moment. Do I detect a shift? A movement? I open my bag again and prise out the green-and-grey packet and swallow the last two diarrhoea pills.

'Here you are!' Lockie jumps on me as soon as I return to the marquee. 'Where did you disappear to?'

He's got me clamped. Hands roam over my butt, snaking for my hem. I bat them away.

After the last twenty minutes on the blue-water loo, I'm not that keen on my ex sticking his hand in my pants. So I wriggle away from him onto the dance floor.

63

''Nother Red Bull?' Lockie says a while later. I'm exhausted. Always tired at the moment. I down mine. And allow him to wind his arms around me as a slow dance comes on. 'So happy we're together again, Frey-Frey,' Lockie says, resting his chin on my shoulder. He's wrecked. But I don't have the energy to be his leaning post tonight. I back him up towards a seating area made of straw bales.

I'm really feeling sick now. 'We're not back together, Lockie,' I say lightly. 'This is just a party thing.' What if that blood isn't piles? Maybe I should get Mum to book a doc's appointment on Monday.

Lockie's practically lying on top of me now, kissing my neck, feeling my boobs.

'I'm really hot,' I say, feeling dizzy.

'Smokin' hot, babe.'

'Can we get some air?'

'Hell, yeah!' He rolls off me and pulls me up onto my fringed cowboy boots. We stotter for the open doors. I see the flashing disco lights, feel my eyes roll back and my head smack the marquee's floorboards.

CHAPTER 10

I wake scratching at my flange. It's pretty bloomin' itchy.
I struggle up to sitting, and realise Mel's upright in her bed
too, watching me.

I self-consciously arrange my flimsy pillow as a buffer
between the wooden-barred headboard and my protruding
vertebrae, and she's still staring. So I wave awkwardly.

She doesn't react. Is she sleeping with her eyes open?
Is she meditating? Should I speak? Instead I say brightly,
'Morn-ing!'

She jumps and visibly reinhabits her body. 'Morning . . .'

'Sleep okay?' I say, sunshine and light.

'Yeah. Great.'

'Me too!'

I had an utterly crap sleep and my hips and shoulders
hurt but let's just keep future interactions positive with

this chick. Gawd, this flange is itchee . . . I scratch the skin around its edge in the hope that it relays the sensation to the untouchable skin below the base station. 'I didn't hear you come in last night,' I try.

'Cool,' she says absently, and leans back to crack a massive yawn herself. 'Keep it down when you're dressing, will you? I need more kip.' She rolls over and pulls her duvet up over her shoulder. 'Just don't tell my mum I was up and down through the night, yeah? And don't tell her I'm skipping breakfast.'

I sat for at least a minute wondering whether I'd just been trumped with the ultimate yawn touché, or whether Mel was legit knackered. But she just stayed under her duvet sleeping or pretending to sleep. So I got ready for breakfast quietly like she asked.

And now I'm standing at the rotating toast machine, scratching redundantly at my tummy.

'Morning, Shit Bag!'

I flinch and turn. 'Hi. Morning, Chris.'

'Want to come sit with us?' He waves his thumb in the general direction of *over there*.

'Eh, yeah. Who's us?' I look back to the toast machine and my two pieces of toast have already slid out onto the tray. I chuck them on my plate, burning my fingers in the process.

'Me and Mel.'

'Uh, Mel's not coming to breakfast.' Itchy. So bloody itchy. I want to cha-cha-cha on the spot. Or do the twist. Or something similarly writhesome because my stoma's so bloomin' itchy this morning.

'Is she okay?'

'Eh, yeah. Think so. She said she was tired. Well, she yawned at me. Then she told me to keep it down.'

Chris grins, biting his bottom lip. 'She sounds fine.'

'That's one way of describing her.'

He laughs. 'Come on, Shit Bag. That was a bold entrance yesterday.'

Bold? You think? I look back to the empty toaster again so I can break eye contact. There's something about this boy that makes me want to grin back at him. But would I be so bold!

'Guess I'm on my own if you don't want to sit with me . . .' he says.

I look at him afresh, genuinely interested that he'd voice this out loud. 'You not comfortable with your own company?' I deadpan.

Eyebrows sky high, he says, 'Nah, Shit Bag, I'm generally at peace with myself. How about you?'

I look away, scan the crowd and spot Cody comparing jam choices, holding two pots up to the light as if they're fossilised amber. 'Can Cody come sit with us too?'

'Course.'

Owen – the Welsh boy who sat on my other side during the icebreaker – has just joined us with his cereal and orange juice, and not long before that, little Jessica and Henners insisted on sitting with me too (this is where all the cool kids hang out, apparently), when Mel's mum appears. 'Good to see you mixing, Freya. All okay?'

'Um, well . . .' There's a collective positive rumble from the others, which shuts me up. So instead of imparting my itchy woes, I make do with surreptitiously digging my elbow into the sticky adhesive flange of my bag. Whatever's going on under there, it's driving me nuts.

Chris says, 'What's our first activity this morning, Annabelle?'

'Bit of Go-Ape climbing for Jessica and Henry. And team building for you big ones.' She taps the side of her nose. 'Can't tell you more than that at this stage. Although, I'm about to allocate teams. Do you four want to work together?'

'What about Mel?' I say, planning some friendship building. 'Can she come in our team too?'

'Where *is* Mel?' Annabelle says. 'She's not still in bed, is she?'

'Uh, no . . .' I falter. 'She's at the loo, I think.'

Chris gives me the wide blue-green eyes and briefly shakes his head.

'How long has she been in the loo?' Annabelle says. 'Is she okay, Chris?'

'Yeah. She's actually gone to get showered,' Chris lies. 'We went for a run first thing.'

'Really? Oh, that's great she's running again. Well done, Chris!'

Chris pulls a joyless smile, but Annabelle doesn't seem to notice.

Like a looping sound clip, I say, 'So can she come in our team too?'

'I'm afraid not, Freya. We have even numbers so it's four in a team. There will be plenty of opportunity to hang out together later though.' She beams at me. I set about biting the loose skin around my thumb.

'Must dash. Chris, tell Mel she can pick her team, but you four go together because I want an even distribution of ages. You and Mel each head up a team separately. Okay?'

Chris shrugs. 'Fine by me.'

'Good, good. You can convince her of that then. Round up for nine thirty a.m. in the common room and we'll have your activity sheets ready.'

'Sure.'

'Jessica, Henry, I'll see you with your mummies and daddies after breakfast.' She waves.

'Annabelle!' I blurt, stopping her in her tracks. 'Could I maybe speak to you after breakfast?'

She checks her watch again. 'You can, but I've an appointment in four minutes. So if it's not urgent . . . ?'

'Right, it's probably—' I catch the others staring and listening. They pretend to focus on their breakfasts, except for Jessica, who's watching me like a hawk. 'Maybe at lunchtime then?' I say. Ha! See, everyone, it's not that urgent. I can wait till lunchtime. Can I wait till lunchtime?

'Are you sure it'll keep?'

No. 'Sure!' I fight the urge to twerk away from my itch. 'Yeah, lunch'll be perfect.' I bite into a rejected toast crust and look at the others with nonchalant raised eyebrows as if to say, *So what's everyone at? Anything interesting going on other than you lot staring at me, listening to my business?*

It appears to work because Annabelle says, 'Good, good. Let's catch up at lunchtime.' And she's gone.

The others are silent for a bit. Until Jessica pipes up. 'I can help you with your ostomy if you'd like, Freya?'

'Uh, thanks, Jessica. It's not that. I just needed to speak to her about something else.'

Humiliating.

Saying you want to see the stoma nurse is like declaring

70

you need to buy diarrhoea pills or saying you need the loo and then waddling from the room with your hand clamped to your nether regions. It's inevitably to do with poo and that's not a great opener when you're pitching your brand to prospective besties.

I try to distract them by saying to Chris, 'Do you think Mel will mind not going in your team?'

Chris makes an incredulous face. 'Why do you say that?'

I shrug and bite my bottom lip. 'Is everything okay with her?'

'Eh, yeah?'

'Her mum sounded worried.'

'She's a parent. Their go-to mode is worried.'

True. I nod. We eat in companionable silence.

'Do you know what Mel eats for breakfast?'

Chris squints. 'Toast? Peanut butter! She likes smooth peanut butter.'

My breakfast peace offering *sort of* worked with Mel – she ate the toast and said thanks. But when she found out she and Chris weren't allowed in the same team she had an argument with her mum and stormed off with her consolation team in tow. Seems Miss Judgy Long Legs has a short fuse. Perhaps we really can be friends.

'Right, let's get this show on the road,' Chris says, waving our activity sheets to direct us outside.

'How far away from the lodge is the activity?' Cody says, flushing pink. She tries to run her fingers through her extensions but her hand sort of stops like it's hit a roadblock. I wonder if her real hair would look that bad? Probably not as bad as mine right now.

'Not sure. There's a map . . .' Chris says, looking through the instructions.

My hand self-consciously prods my own fine frizz. The hair on my head started falling out a couple of weeks ago. And, bizarrely, at the same time tiny dark hairs appeared on my body, even my tummy. It's all the weight loss apparently. Beverley says your system goes into crisis mode. The tiny hairs on my torso are to keep me warm because I'm so emaciated, like insulation. My body just knew to grow them. How weird is that! Though I hope to every deity in the universe that my body knows to stop. Right now. I do not need to add Wolf Girl to my repertoire of nicknames. And then there are the periods. Or lack of them. I imagine you're thinking, *How can you complain about that?* Well, yeah, it's pretty convenient that I don't have them, but it doesn't really make you feel very womanly. I feel like I've regressed to a pre-teen. Even my boobs have shrunk away with my weight.

'We're going about five hundred metres . . .' Chris says.

Cody side-eyes Owen and blushes a deeper pink.

Oh, I see. 'Yeah, if we need the loo . . .' I lift my eyebrows at Chris, hoping he understands what I'm trying to insinuate without me having to shout: *I think Cody might be worried about needing the loo!* God, this is the most ridiculous camp I've ever been to! What am I talking about, this is the *only* camp I've ever been to – because I'm missing hockey camp, in *Portugal*, with my real friends!

It's still ridiculous. How the hell did they think this would work? We should've stayed in the city somewhere. What's the point of dangling mountain air and open spaces all around us when we're too frightened to stray far from modern-day plumbing?

'Let's be clear,' Chris says, cutting through my garbled thoughts.

Oh, I've just realised that I've not scratched my bag for the last two minutes. I might just make it until lunchtime. Hurray.

Itchy!

Jeez, it's psychosomatic. It must be. If I just don't think about it . . .

'We've all got issues with our guts. Let's not be embarrassed about that. It's why we're here. So if we need the toilet, just say. No biggy. No stress. In fact, I'm going to go right now. Anyone else? No? Well, if you can take the instructions for me, Cody, maybe you can all wait outside?'

Aww, I'm really starting to like this boy. 'Actually, guys, I need the loo as well,' I say, seeing Cody share a smile with Owen. 'Won't be long.'

CHAPTER 11

I'm in the loos now. Okay, I'll admit it. I might be okay here.

Obviously, I'd rather be in Portugal. But it's not like I've had much in the way of communication. Just the heart emoji Morven replied with when I said I hoped they'd arrived safe. Zero messages this morning. And Portugal's the same time zone as the UK!

As for Lockie, I found a picture earlier posted by one of the lads I still follow: he's in his boxers, with bed hair and midway through cleaning his teeth. It gave me crippling stomach cramps, only now I don't have a large intestine I can't blame that on bad digestion.

I straight up miss Lockie. Miss everyone. Everything. Hockey. The team . . . But apparently they don't miss me.

Quit simping! I'm turning soft. What do I care if they don't message me? It'll be the usual pity messages from

Morven, and detachment from Suriya. I'm losing my focus because of this poxy camp. I need to endure this hellhole, not enjoy it. And if I inadvertently learn about the pouch from Mel in the process, that's an unexpected bonus. One step closer to returning to my real life, with my real friends and Lockie. Because that's the objective. Get this bag reversed, get rid of Shit Bag, and everything goes back to the way it was. The way it *should* be. When I'm Freya again.

So I don't need to speak to Lockie or Morven or Suriya until I'm ready to live. This place is just a sort of stasis. Purgatory. Itchy purgatory.

I screw up my eyes for a moment and lift the hem of my vest top. There's a red circle all the way around the sticky peachy-skin-coloured flange. Am I poisoned? Maybe that's why I'm going soft in the head. Or . . . actually it's probably because I've been scratching so much. Yep, these look like nail marks. Oh well, just another two hours until lunchtime. I can wait two hours.

I go through my usual process: empty bag, clean the end, flush, wash my hands and . . . pause in front of the mirror. I could've put eyeliner on this morning. Mascara. Over the last few weeks, I've lost my mojo. My dignity. Look at me. All bony cheekbones like a skeleton with skin. And my eyes all starey. I'm going to have to cut my hair shorter. There's just enough for a stubby ponytail but it's so thin and wispy it's a token pretence at femininity. I look like a brunette Owen. Do I? Probably. Maybe I should buy another bra. This stretchy thing, below my grey sleeveless vest, doesn't really fit. I should've got something more . . . I dunno. Just more. But then most of my underwire bras, despite being too loose, hurt my ribs. I dry my hands on my jeans. They're far too baggy. My cinched belt with all its extra holes is the only thing holding up my dignity. I did bring shorts. But there's no way I'm wearing them, even though it looks hot outside. No way anyone is seeing underneath. My pins. My bones.

I push out through the door and almost walk into Chris.

'You alright?' he says.

'Yeah, fine.' I cross my arms self-consciously.

'Thought I'd give Cody and Owen a bit of time alone.'

He saw the chemistry too then. 'Alright, Mr Matchmaker!'

'I think she's going through a hard time of it,' he says.

I follow his attention out through the window and see Cody sitting cross-legged on the grass, smiling at Owen. 'You think or you know?'

Chris looks at me sharply, his dark eyebrows flicking up. 'I know,' he says.

I nod. 'Okay.'

We're all flanged then.

* * *

'Your physical challenge for today is to build a team castle,' Cody reads aloud.

It's moments like this that I wish I had Mum's single-eyebrow-raising gene. Instead, I have to scrunch my nose to show my distaste.

'I think they mean a den,' Chris says.

'Out of what?' I say.

'Everything we need is down there at the opposite end of the loch,' Cody relays from the instructions.

'Course it is . . . You okay to go there?' I murmur to Cody so Owen doesn't hear, 'I've got loperamide if you want some?'

'It's alright,' she whispers back. 'I took some with my prednisolone after breakfast.'

I nod like I know what that is. Like I understand the implications of what's wrong with her. Is it rude to ask more? Or worse not to ask? This whole place is seriously messed up.

We troop down the path and along the stones and mossy, weedy edge of the lapping water. It's rough footings. We say nothing all the way. I don't have the breath for it, and I guess Chris and Owen aren't talkers. As for Cody . . . Well, I've been watching her intermittently as I attempt to not break an ankle or fall on my face and it seems Cody is, without question, in crush mode. She only has eyes for Owen.

At about two on the lake's clock face – if this clock happened to be in a Dali painting and had melted into a squiggly oblong – we skirt round a jutting spit of trees with their roots exposed. Black peaty soil washes down to the loch, dredged along with a trickling burn. Someone's driven sawn-off telegraph posts into the ground as a barrier round the trees. I guess, so we don't go investigate and get totalled by a landslide. The others cross the burn's footbridge, and I lean on its handrail because I have a stitch.

'You alright?' Chris calls back to me.

'Yeah. Just, a stone in my trainer,' I lie, and trudge on.

I'm quietly wheezing by the time we hit the sandy beach. It's such an incongruous sight that I imagine a giant plesiosaur must have taken a chomp from the forest edge as it headed north for Loch Ness. There's a grassy flat just above the beach with two log cabins and picnic tables, and behind that a car park and a single-track access road snaking up the hill beyond. Perhaps this place isn't as badly planned out after all. At least if we end up injured the ambulance can get to us.

Mel's already here with her team, dragging apart a massive, untorched pyre of wooden pallets, ropes, hammers, nails, floorboards, tarpaulins, poles and tent pegs. And their 'castle' is taking shape. Well, they've propped three pallets against one another and put another on the top for a roof.

Out of the corner of my eye, I watch Chris walk over to Mel.

'Are they judging us?' Owen says.

I'm glad to hear I'm not the only competitive one in the team.

I look to Cody. 'What did the instructions say?'

'It's our den for the week,' she says. 'Our team meeting place.'

'Like a little kids' gang hut?' I say, using my nose-scrunch again.

Chris laughs at something Mel says and collapses comfortably onto the ground beside her.

Distracted by their familiarity, I say, 'Are you sure we didn't get the little kids' instructions?'

Cody prongs her snarled hair with her fingers. 'I don't know. Might be quite nice to have somewhere private to get away from our parents.' And her eyes slide to Owen.

I stop myself from snorting like a prepubescent boy who's just heard the word 'boobs'. I wonder if Owen's aware that Cody's imagining playing queen of the castle and already cast Owen as her lowly serving swain. (That's the male version of a wench, in case you were wondering. We're all about equality in this imaginary queendom.)

The three of us go to the pile of materials and I pull half-heartedly at a pallet. After I budge it about a metre, I say, 'Slight problem . . . My scar. I'm not supposed to do any heavy lifting.' Who the hell designed this bloody camp?

Mel's mum.

'Oh no, Freya!' Cody gushes in her sweet way. 'Chris and Owen can do the heavy lifting. You should sit down and rest.'

Seizing my opportunity, I point to Chris and Mel, still chatting. 'I'll just go ask him to come help.'

'Hey,' I say, smiling at Mel and then at their den. 'Like what you've done with your place. Spacious.'

She pouts and lifts her head in a reverse nod, and says in a cool deadpan, 'It'll look bigger once the furniture's in.'

I grin, but apparently that's all I'm getting back. 'Sorry to interrupt,' I say carefully. 'But I can't lift heavy stuff because of my scar, so can you . . .'

'Oh shit, course!' Chris gets up.

'Speak later, Chris,' Mel says, brutally insinuating she's not planning on speaking to *me* later. This bird sure knows how to hold a grudge. She couldn't just forgive and forget already and tell me all about her pouch and how to fast-track mine? No? That *really* a big ask? I mean, I brought her toast!

81

CHAPTER 12

My team don't seem to mind that I can't pull my weight physically. Which is really nice of them. If I'm honest, it's not what I'm used to and it makes me feel weirdly grateful. A sensation I'm probably not that familiar with either. I guess I suit the name Shit Bag in more ways than one.

So we plan out our castle together. And settle on the need for twelve pallets, one central support pole and a tarpaulin. Chris starts off all butch lifting a couple of pallets in each arm. But then changes his mind and carries just one under each armpit. And Cody and Owen carry one together.

I collect the ropes and nails. And try to make light of my uselessness by pretending the claw hammer is Thor's Mjölnir and is unmoveable due to my unworthiness. I dig my toes into the sand and mime pulling hard at the wooden handle.

Chris comes over and stands with his hands on his hips, watching me.

'It's not heavy or anything,' I explain. 'I'm just unworthy.'

Chris pouts and nods.

'Fancy a go?'

'Nah. Try a bit harder. If you manage, I'll call you The Mighty Shit Bag. But Jane ended up in Valhalla, remember.'

'Oh shit! Here. You take it then.'

'No chance. It's all yours.'

I swing the hammer over my shoulder and grin at him. He's passed the Marvel test.

Just so you know, I am not a simpering little weakling. I used to be really strong. I'm the naturally sporty one out of me and the girls. The first one to get into the senior hockey squad. Well, I was . . . I suppose I've lost my place now. No matter how positive the surgeon and Beverley are, telling me I'll be able to do *anything I want*. I'm thinking that's a PR move on their part. They've got to keep me positive. They're not going to have many future customers if they're all doom and gloom, now, are they?

It's almost midday and there's half an hour until lunchtime. We're taking a water break before we finish off our roof.

We've gone for a hexagonal big top, tent-castle sort of thing – each wall's two pallets wide. After we're rehydrated, we plan to raise the mast in the middle and drape tarpaulin over the top like a tepee.

As it's getting really warm, I suggested we keep the join in the tarpaulin openable. That way we can flip the lid back like a skylight and let the cool air circulate, rather than roast inside like chickens in an oven.

'Just a bit more,' I say, digging my nails deeper into the sand and silt trench. It's wet at the bottom. 'Do you think we should put stones in the base? As foundations? Otherwise the pole might sink.'

Chris is hugging the tall support pole so it doesn't topple and break the walls. 'Is it bad if it sinks?' he says.

I sit back on my bony bum. My knees are aching. 'Dunno. Might sink unevenly.'

'I'll get some,' Owen says.

'Me too,' says Cody.

Owen and Cody head off with the bucket they've been using to lug sand around.

My bag's itching incessantly now. I think it's because I'm sweating with the heat and the effort of digging holes and filling in. I rub the area beside my bag with my elbow because my hands are wet and sandy.

'Looks alright,' Chris says, glancing over to the other constructions. In our – completely unbiased – opinion we've created the most robust, architecturally sound structure of the three. The team to our left built a haphazard maze of tunnels and tents like a giant hamster's run, and Mel's team have built a glorified, two-pallets-high bus shelter with a tarpaulin roof. They've been paddling in the loch for the last twenty minutes. I'm starting to think that girl's got her priorities straight in life.

'Is this enough?' Cody says, as she and Owen drag the full bucket of stones back inside our den.

'That's loads.' I tip a few into the hole and bed out the base of my quicksand trench. 'Right.' I nod to Chris.

He pauses. 'Thinking about this . . . we should put the tarpaulin over the top of the pole before we fix it upright. We won't be able to do it after.'

'Good thinking.' Me and the other two trudge outside, grab the tarpaulin and drag it over the sand. Just outside the pallet walls, I freeze. I feel curiously free. A sensation of weightlessness. An unburdening.

'You okay?' Cody says.

I'm a statue. I don't dare even look towards the others. My hands still grip the tarpaulin.

'Chris?' Cody says.

'What?'

'Freya. She's . . .' I can hear the unease in Cody's voice.

'What's up? Everything alright?'

It can't be. It *can't* be. I move my hand from the tarpaulin and edge my thumb under my vest top. Wet. Sweat. It's sweat. I look down at my thumb, but there's sand all over it. *Can't tell.* I flare my nostrils.

'Freya?'

Chris says something like, 'Wait. I need to put this . . .'

I lift my thumb to my nose and smell. *Oh – God. Oh – GOD. Oh my fucking GOD!! OH – U-H-H!* Can't breathe. Breathe can't. Hand. Don't. Don't want hand.

'Chris, do something! Freya?'

'No!' I heave. 'Don't come any— Stay away! Stay there. All of you! In fact, turn around. Cody. Owen! Turn around. Don't look at me.'

Cody sticks her hands up as if I'm holding a gun on her and turns away from me. I'm crying now. 'Ngeeaaa!' High-pitched squeal. 'Guh-hu!' Retching. 'Gu!' Worse. Clamp mouth shut. Screwed-up face crying.

'What's wrong with her? Chris! Help her.'

'Freya?' Chris approaches me.

'Stay there!' I can't move. I don't even dare point at him. I let go of the tarpaulin with my left hand so that I at least have the use of it. I'll never write again. I don't want my right hand anymore. 'Stop looking at me.' I close my eyes. I can't bear it. I'm blubbering, my stomach muscles are juddering and that's making it even worse.

'Freya?'

'Nnhe?'

'Tell me right now what's wrong or I'm going to have to look.'

'No! Away.' Oh God, I can smell it. I can smell it. I put my left hand over my face. And say, 'My bag!'

CHAPTER 13

'Your bag?'

'Off!'

'It's fallen off?'

'Nmghh!'

'Right. Okay. But you're not hurt?'

'No. It's fucking fallen off. Off. OFFF!'

Cody's hyperventilating now.

'Okay. Cody, calm down. Don't you get upset too. She'll be fine. Owen, take Cody and go for a walk along the sand. I'll sort this out. Okay?'

'I'll get my mum and da—'

'No! Don't.' *Don't you bloody dare tell anyone.* I clench my jaw. 'Don't let her tell anyone,' I hiss at Chris.

'Cody, I'll sort it out. But this isn't for us to tell other people. Okay?'

'No. Of – course. I won't.'

'This has happened to me loads of times,' Chris tells Cody with a wave of his hand. 'It's no big deal.'

'No big deal? NO BIG DEAL!'

'FREYA!' Chris shouts at me so forcefully that I shut my mouth and whimper. 'You're not hurt. I thought you'd hurt yourself. In fact, Cody, Owen, why don't you go ahead to lunch. Look, the others are going too.' They slope away, Cody glancing reluctantly over her shoulder at me.

I scowl and twist my lips in a snivelly snarl at Chris.

'Let's get you back to the lodge and you can change it.'

'I'm not going anywhere. If I move, it'll . . .' I decide that standing's too much work under these conditions and let my knees give way. I'm now on my back on the sand. I pull the tarpaulin over me so I can't see what's going on down there. I'll just revert to my norm. Close eyes and someone else can deal with this. I want to die. 'Get the stoma nurse,' I say.

'The stoma nurse?'

'Get her!' I yell.

'Okay! But what about your gear? Where's your stuff?'

'Black rucksack, room ten. Stoma nurse!'

'Look, how are you going to clean yourself up? Just hold it on and we can go up—'

'Get the STOMA NURSE!'

'Okay! Okay.'

I'm lying here with my eyes closed, scrubbing my right hand's fingertips into the sand and breathing through my mouth so that I can't smell it. I'm fine now. Catatonic. No longer in my body. This is not happening to me. It's some sort of alternate imagining of the ninth circle of hell. What comes after that? Is there a tenth? Have I upgraded to a VIP, especially for me, tenth circle of hell?

My phone beeps a fourth time before I finally bring myself to look at it – seriously, *now* it starts working! Perhaps I'm actually in a dream and it's my alarm waking me up and if I just look at the phone I'll snap out of this nightmare. It'll be morning and the last few months will turn out to've been one big, bad dream. You know how time mutates in dreams and what seems like a month's worth of events actually passed in the space of a ten-minute nap? That's what's happening right now. I'm having a ten-minute, diabolical snooze.

I fish my phone out from my pocket with my left hand. Thank God it was in my left pocket. In my right it would be covered.

Dad's messaged me:

I reread the message. I must have sunstroke. Usually he's telling me that there's plenty of time for boyfriends. Like when Lockie and me had our third break-up – I was crying that time – and he said I was far too young to have met the love of my life and there were plenty more fish in the sea. I'd have them falling at my feet. I'd have my pick. Guess that's not the case now I'm damaged goods. He's trying to pair me off with some random guy. With a bag. Like me. Is this some sort of f'ed-up matchmaking camp?

Ugh, I can smell it!

About two days pass before I hear crunching on the distant shingle. Just one person's crunching. And then he's here on the sand.

'Right. No stoma nurse,' Chris says. 'She's sorting out a little kid who fell and banged his stoma on the climbing frame.'

'Nheeea!'

'Stop being so dramatic. It's happened to all of us.'

'I need the stoma nurse! Did you tell her?'

'I left a message for her.'

'I'll wait then. Stay over there. I don't want you to smell me.'

'Are you serious?'

'Yes, I'm serious!' I keep my eyes closed.

I hear a grunt so I assume he sits down where I've instructed. 'At least use these,' he says. 'Or don't! Your choice.'

A plastic-wrapped missile hits my elbow. I look to see he's chucked me a pack of wet wipes with a bin bag loosely knotted round it.

'Oh. Thanks . . .' I wipe both hands. I'm repetitive with my right one. I'm not ready to witness the carnage below the tarpaulin. 'Has yours really fallen off lots of times?'

'That's the least of my worries,' Chris says. 'You must've had a leak by now?'

'No. I haven't.'

'Well, there's a first time for everything.' He doesn't speak for a while and I realise that all I can hear is the distant squeal of a kestrel or something like it.

I ask, 'Where's everyone else?'

'Gone to lunch.'

'You didn't tell them?'

'No. And Cody and Owen promise to keep schtum. Look, there's no point in waiting here for the nurse. I brought your gear and I've got mine too. Why don't you change your bag?'

I don't answer. I just focus on dividing every cell in my body. Like that *Prometheus* film, at the beginning, when the godlike-being divides and crumbles into dust. I wish I was dust. Who knows why I keep referencing *Prometheus*! It just seems very relevant to my life right now.

'Freya?'

'I don't know how!' I snap. 'Okay? Get it? I don't. Know. How to.'

'What do you mean?'

'My mum changes it.'

'Your mum?'

'That's what I said.'

He's quiet for a while and then he sighs. 'Do you want *me* to do it?'

'No! Ugh! Don't be disgusting.' Showing him my guts? That's worse than flashing him my bits!

'I'm trying to help but . . . What do you want me to do?'

'Nothing. I'll just wait.'

After another silence. 'I'm not trying to upset you, but don't you think you should learn to change it?'

'No. I don't have to. I'm getting it reversed in a few months and then I'll be back to normal. No need.'

'Right . . .'

'You've had yours for six months? You must be due to get it reversed.'

'Mine's permanent.'

I stop myself. The knee-jerk, horror-filled parroting of *permanent*? 'Sorry,' I say. 'I didn't know.'

'Don't be. I'm grateful for my bag.'

I don't know what to say to that.

'I'm always going to be a Shit Bag.'

Oh God. This really is Camp Kill Me Now.

CHAPTER 14

'Did you come up with the Shit Bag nickname yourself?' Chris says after a pause.

I open my eyes. 'Yep. All on my ownsome.'

'Thought so.'

'I wasn't calling *you* Shit Bag, you know.'

'Yeah, you said that.'

I look over now. I can see his trainers and bare brown shins. He's resting his arms on his knees. I guess he changed into shorts up at the lodge. I don't blame him. I'm sweating like a pig here. Like a pig in shit. Sweating *and* wallowing in shit like a pig. A Freya pig.

'So why are you encouraging people to call *you* Shit Bag?' Chris says.

'Dunno. It sums up how I feel about myself, I suppose. Why?'

He's slow to reply, but then he says, 'I thought you were

using it to take the power away from it. You know? So other people can't use it against you.'

I wriggle round a bit to try and see his face better. And manage to say, 'Have you been called Shit Bag?'

He grimaces and shrugs. 'It's a rite of passage for people like us.'

I process this revelation – that we've been through similar experiences. The bird of prey *screaks* overhead.

'My mates still call me Shit Bag sometimes,' he elaborates. 'I get it. It's funny. And I know they don't mean it maliciously – well, most of them don't . . .'

I can't be mean to this boy now. He's rolled the mutual Shit Bag nickname out for sympathy votes and one-upped me with a permanent bag. He's trumped me. Although, it smells like I'm the one doing the trumping. I think my body heat is creating a poo miasma. 'Do you want me to stop calling myself Shit Bag around you?' I say.

Again, he doesn't answer immediately. And I experience this weird sensation of freedom while I wait. Like I don't have to think and do and worry and fight the world. While he takes his sweet time, thinking about what I'm going to do next. To be Shit Bag or not to be Shit Bag? That is the question!

Then he says simply, 'No. You can be Shit Bag.' Adding, 'It suits you.'

I gasp. 'So RUDE!' But actually I have this thrilling fizz

in my chest. That I'm not destined to take this all lying down – despite the fact I *am* currently flat-on-my-back lying down covered in my own shit. Turns out this guy isn't the sweet, good-natured pushover he could've been. And I kind of like—

'This is ridiculous,' he says, interrupting my jumbled thoughts. 'Why don't I talk you through the process? Even if your ostomy's temporary you can't keep getting your mum to change your bag.'

I roll my eyes. 'You're a plant, aren't you? My dad paid you to say that. I bet my mum sabotaged this bag – she probably didn't stick it on properly so that this would happen.'

'You got me. Let's see what's in here . . .'

I stretch and strain a look over my shoulder at Chris rifling through my rucksack. I haven't a clue what's in there.

'Good, you have a stoma template.'

'I don't know what that means,' I say.

'It's so you know what size to cut the hole in the flange. To fit over your stoma?'

I twist my lips and shake my head.

Chris frowns at me and says, 'Right. I get it. Little princess leaves it *all* to Mummy.'

'Insult me all you like.'

'Look, sorry. I get tetchy when I'm hungry.'

'Hey, I'm not stopping you. Leave me a bottle of water and go get your lunch.'

96

'I'm not *leaving* you here!' he laughs incredulously.

I flick my eyebrows to myself, acknowledging that he's kinda passing the vibe check.

'I'd usually get straight in the shower and clean myself up first,' he mutters.

'I'll shower when I go back.'

'And the edge of your new flange will swell and get sticky with the water . . .'

'Well, yeah . . .'

'And itchy. Don't you find that maddeningly itchy after a shower?'

This I *can* answer, but I'm not telling the truth, that's for sure. I can't admit that I'll often go a day or two without a shower for that very reason. Okay, I'm a stinking beast! And I *may not* have had a proper shower this morning. I have this trick where I just sort of direct the jet strategically at certain creases in my body. And I wash my hair so everyone thinks I have incredibly average, and normal, personal hygiene standards.

'Are you sure you don't want to just go up to the lodge holding something over your stoma?'

'Very sure!'

'What about the showers here then?'

'Where?'

'The cabins with the toilets. I showed you on the map.'

'No, you didn't!'

'Oh, I told Cody and Owen.'

I close my eyes, inhale deeply to psych myself up – immediately regret it as the poo vapour is rising – and gasp, 'Fine, I'll shower here!'

'Great. Have some of these first then,' he says all businesslike.

Another bag lands by my shoulder. I reach for it and discover it's a packet of marshmallows. 'I'm not sure this is a good time to eat.'

'It's a trick. Marshmallows slow down your guts. Eat a few now, and when you put the bag on in ten to fifteen minutes your stoma will've gone quiet.'

'Hmm! Did *you* come up with that?'

'No, my stoma nurse.'

'Bet you have a nice one. Mine hates me.'

'I wonder why.'

'Excuse me! Feed me marshmallows then.'

'Uhh . . . Okay, if that's what you're into.'

I bite the inside of my mouth to stop myself grinning. And explain, 'My hands feel dirty still.'

'Ah.' He seems to take great pleasure in stuffing two pink and two white marshmallows into my mouth in quick succession. 'I'll check out the showers while you do a quick clean-up. Hold your bag on over your stoma when you walk up to the cabin.'

Chris leaves before I can object.

I wonder if this is similar to when you fall and break something and you go into shock. You can't feel the pain, but you know something really bad is going on down below. Who am I kidding? This is nothing like an injury. I've just got poo on me, for God's sake. Babies do it every day. I did it every day when I was a baby. Ironically, Mum said I was potty-trained at nine months. Perhaps this is the universe saying it was too early and I need to regress.

Come on, Freya, you can do this!

I lift the tarpaulin, and my vest top. There's a yellow-green tidemark along my stomach just above the waistband of my jeans. I probably shouldn't've had that glass of orange juice at breakfast. Maybe that's why this happened? No. It started getting itchy through the night. I look at the sky and wipe, and stuff it in the bin bag. I undo my belt, pull it completely off, chuck it out of the way and undo my jeans button and zip. I'm grateful they're so loose. It means I can easily push them down onto my hips. They're not actually that dirty. There's a sort of green-brown mark on the inside of my right-hand pocket and at the waist. My black pants, however, are soaked. On a plus, it appears these good old M&S multipack boy shorts have done a sterling job of mopping up and containing the situation. In fact – sod it! I'm getting up and dealing with this in the shower. I feel for the hard plastic ring where the bag connects with the flange and grip it through my soggy pants, so that I'm holding everything in the correct general vicinity. And stand. My jeans promptly fall down to my knees. 'For crying out!' I manage to wrangle them back up and waddle – gripping jeans, bin bag and ostomy bag – up the beach, across the grass and to Chris and the log cabins. 'What's the verdict on the showers?' I shout.

'Shit Bag! Fancy seeing you here,' he says brightly.

'Showers?'

'High-five?' He holds his hand up, waiting for my celebratory slap.

I scowl at him. *Is he messing?*

He widens his grin. And his eyes flick down to clock my stooped kind-of-got-my-hands-full-right-now situation, gripping my bag with one hand and my sagging jeans and the bin bag with the other. And he laughs. 'No high-five?' he checks.

'No,' I say, feeling both exasperated and just a bit impressed that he can keep up his good humour. I'm tempted to sling my bag – which is still relatively full of sloshing poo – at him.

'About the showers,' he says. 'There's one outside the Ladies and one outside the Gents. But . . . Well, take a look for yourself.'

I shuffle round the side of the Ladies. Wooden slats surround only three sides of the cubicle like a gappy garden fence, and it's open at the front. 'Bollocks.'

'Never fear! I think I have an ingenious solution.' He's still grinning, and it's now so wide his face might actually split. And he jogs, all bouncy and positive, back down to our den.

I take the opportunity to shuffle to the Ladies to empty my bag – bit late for that really but anyway – and when I come back out, still gripping my bag and flange over my stoma, I see he's returned with my rucksack, his bag of kit and, dragging behind him, the tarpaulin we were going to use for the roof. I watch him wrap the tarpaulin around the whole shower box and tuck it over the top of the walls so that it doesn't slip down.

'See, especially for you.' He flaps the overlap open at the front like a door – like we'd planned for the skylight of our den.

I grin back. 'You, my friend, are a genius.'

'In you get then.'

I duck inside the shower and once I've checked there aren't any gaps Chris can see in through, I take off my jeans. I slowly ease the front of my pants away, grab my empty bag and shove it into the bin liner. I peel off the pants and bung them in the bag too.

My vest top hasn't fared as well as I thought, probably because I was lying nearly flat on the sand – not the brightest idea in hindsight. 'Can I borrow your T-shirt?'

'I got you these.' His hand dangles over the top of the

partition, offering me denim cut-off shorts and a baby-pink T-shirt.

Shocked, I take the clothes and stare at them. 'Where did you get these?'

'Your suitcase.'

'You went into my suitcase?' A visual catalogue of everything embarrassing in there flashes through my head: emergency tampons in case my period comes back, pants, a couple of greyish bras . . . Nibblet!

'What was the alternative? Leave you in shitty jeans?'

I exhale through my nostrils and say, 'Did you bring underwear?'

'Uhh . . . I wasn't sure. So . . .' His hand reappears, and pincered delicately between his forefinger and thumb are . . . a pair of my bright-pink boy-shorts knickers and my old blush-pink Nike sports bra.

I take them.

'Is that okay?' I hear the anxiety in his voice.

'Eh, yeah. Thanks.' I don't know how I feel about this. I'm embarrassed. But also, I'm not . . . I tuck all the clothes in a gap between the wooden slats so they stay dry and realise what it is that's intrigued me. 'Did you match my underwear to my T-shirt?'

There's silence. Then he says, 'Is that not right?'

'No. Yeah. It's good!' I say quickly, feeling that weird

102

fizzing sensation of excitement in my chest again. 'Right! Shall we get my bag changed?'

So, to cut a long story very slightly shorter, Chris grabs me some soap from the loos and I clean myself up in the best, and definitely the most liberating, shower I've had in my entire life. Because not only am I open to the elements and just a sheet of blue tarpaulin away from a guy, but also this is the first time in seven weeks I've bathed without my bag. And even better, the marshmallows do their job. My stoma barely moves the whole time I'm washing myself. So I don't even have to look at it. I just pretend that the knobbly, protruding thing isn't there on my belly. Hey, leave me to my delusions!

'Are you ready?' Chris calls out from the other side of the tarpaulin.

'Ugh!' I turn off the shower. 'I suppose so,' I say reluctantly. 'Yes, I'm ready.'

I've not really told you much about the stoma. Other than I hate looking at it. But I guess the time has come to tell all.

Well, the end of my small intestine – the bit they sort of roll out on itself like rolling up the bottom of your jeans and then stitching that outer part of the hem to your belly so it doesn't go anywhere – looks just like a strawberry-coloured sea anemone. Or the neck of a red, latex-covered, chunky-knit polo neck for Barbie. Honestly. It's the most bizarre-looking thing you've ever seen in your entire life. It really does look alien. I've got super-pale skin on my tummy too, so the contrast is pretty extreme. Anyway. Now that I've binned my old bag and I've had a great time washing myself I see exactly why I've been itching all morning. There's a red rash on my skin tracking out below my stoma at your seven on the clock, if you were standing looking at me. Which you're not – thank God! 'My skin's raw,' I say.

'What kind of raw? Is it weepy?'

'Raised and red where it's been itching.'

'Yeah, your poo's been leaking under the flange. That'll be why the bag fell off. Does your mum usually put paste around the hole?'

I don't really want to be called a princess again. 'Umm, have you got any more of those marshmallows?'

'Why? Is your stoma moving? Here, wrap some tissue around it.'

'No . . . I was going to say I don't know if Mum uses paste, but I wanted you to eat some marshmallows beforehand, so you don't bite my head off again.'

'You're funny. Okay, wipe your skin around the stoma with this.' His hand comes in through the door offering me a little alcohol wipe sachet. I take it, and he adds. 'It's going to hurt like sulphuric acid on the raw bit, but you want it to be clean.'

'Really? You couldn't have lied to me?'

'You've reminded me I'm hungry. You deserve it.'

'Ngahh! That flippin STINGGS!'

'Good,' he says.

Good?

And in comes a little white bottle and the flange. 'Now, puff that powder on lightly. All over the bits that are itching but not too much . . . and hold the flange in front of your stoma. Does the hole in the middle look a similar size? Like it would slide snugly over the stoma?'

'Yes.'

'Cool. Hand it back to me. Okay, I'm going to peel off the backing and put paste around the hole to make a secure seal. When I hand it in, try not to smear the paste everywhere.' He carefully passes the pre-pasted flange back through the tarpaulin flap. 'Got it?'

'Yep.'

'Now fit the sticky doughnut over your stoma. The hole I cut should be a perfect fit. And push down on every bit of the flange so it sticks evenly to your tummy. No air pockets. That way you won't get leaks underneath.'

After a lot of prodding and smoothing I think I've done it. 'Now what?'

'Don't bend too much. It'll take about an hour to really stick. Here . . .' He hands in a fresh bag. 'I've closed the clip on the bottom already. Line up the two plastic rings – the one on the bag over the one on the flange – and then when you're happy it's snapped together, you clip the little latch at the side of the bag and that locks the two parts together securely.'

'Sorted. Now what?'

'Now you get dressed.'

'What? Am I *done*?'

'You're done.'

'But. That was easy!'

'Yes, Shit Bag. It *is* easy!'

'Alright, alright, I see that now,' I mutter, as I wipe myself dry with the clean leg of my jeans. And marvel again at the matchy-matchiness of the pink on pink on pink collection of clothes Chris has brought me.

'You okay in there?' he asks after a little while. 'You're being very *quiet* for you, Shit Bag.'

'I was just thinking it's a shame you *aren't*!' I clapback. 'Being quiet.'

'Unnecessary! Here I am doing charity work, missing my lunch for you.'

Charity? 'I'm doing *fine*, thank you very much, *Chris*! Thank you for asking. Better than fine actually.'

I open the tarpaulin and smile at him, blinking and fluttering my eyelashes all ladylike. 'Thank you for your charity work!'

He laughs. 'You're very welcome, charity case.'

I stick my tongue out at him good-naturedly.

Chris takes the bin bag and knots it for me, while I roll up my dirty clothes and quickly wash my hands under the shower.

'You happy with how your bag looks?' he asks when we're all done. 'How it's sticking?'

I must be in some sort of euphoric high because I just pull up my pink T-shirt and show him my bag. No drama. 'What do you think?'

He presses it gently with his fingers. 'Looks alright.'

'Looks *alright*? This is the best-applied ileostomy bag that's ever been,' I say, hamming it up, adding, 'I had an excellent teacher!' I'm actually genuinely proud of myself. Of both of us. He *is* an excellent teacher.

Chris grins and offers me a bottle of water and the packet of marshmallows. 'To celebrate,' he says, and sits on the step.

I thought he'd be rushing up to the canteen to see if there's any food left, but I'm happy to sit with him in the afterglow of a successful life achievement. I sit, clink my water bottle against his and wish him good health. '*Slàinte Mhath.*'

CHAPTER 15

My phone beeps. I have two missed calls from Morven and an old-school *text* of all things. She's sent me a pic of her in our yellow training gear – her face is beetroot, she's got sweat dripping down her face and her hair's turned to strawberry-blonde fluff around her temples. Her message says:

> **Morven:** Hope you're having more fun than me. Let me know when I can call you later xx.

Biting my lip, I type a reply:

> **Me:** I've just had a naked outdoor shower with a guy from Merchants!

and wave my phone around to try for some reception, but there's nothing. I think better of broadcasting such inflammatory gossip and delete the message.

'What are you laughing at?' Chris says smiling.

'Nothing. I wasn't laughing . . .' I turn my phone face down on the step. But I can't stop a smile creeping across my mouth, imagining the fireworks that message would induce if I actually sent it. 'You go to Merchants . . .' I say.

'You *know* Merchants?' He looks down at what he's wearing, probably for a tell-tale logo.

'You were wearing your school tracksuit yesterday,' I explain.

He nods. 'Where do *you* go to school?'

'Lowettsons.'

'Ahh! Do you . . . ?' He's laughing and shaking his head.

'Yes. I do.'

'Sorry. I don't mean to laugh. Well, do you know what we call Lowettsons girls?'

'Do I want to know?'

'It's not bad. I mean . . .'

That's what you say when it *is* bad. I'm sort of ready for violence.

'Um, we call you Sweets. You know, short for sweethearts?'

Not trusting that this really is as sweet as he's claiming, I say, 'Right?'

'But you're also hard. So we call you Hard Boiled Sweets.'

'You call us *hard boiled sweets*?' I say, looking and sounding unimpressed by Merchants' utterly rubbish nickname for the girls at my school.

'It's because of your uniforms,' Chris adds.

'Ah! I get it. Okay. Amusing,' I say, deadpan. Our school ties and sports kits have yellow and pink stripes. I narrow my eyes, imagining the other things they say about us if they're calling us boiled sweets. 'So what about the Lowettsons boys? Are they hard boiled sweets too?'

'No!' He laughs and rubs the back of his neck.

'Well, what do you call the boys?'

'We call them Flumps.' He looks at me now, biting the side of his bottom lip, like he's not sure whether he should elaborate.

'Flumps? As in the pink-and-yellow-striped marshmallow sweets?'

'Exactly! Because your rugby team's soft like marshmallows.'

'Oyy! We beat you last year—!' I punch him on the arm.

'See! Hard Boiled. You're reverting to violence!' He rubs his arm but he's still laughing. 'The only reason you beat our Firsts was because I was ill.'

'Uh, big-headed, much?'

'No. Fact.' He chucks a pink marshmallow in the air and catches it in his mouth. I know I'm shit at doing that so I don't embarrass myself trying. I bite mine in half and wonder if Lockie and the rugby team know that Merchants call them Flumps. I have a little chuckle to myself.

'So you were in the Firsts?' I say, shaking off my tension as I chew.

'I should be next season again too.'

I stop chewing, shocked, before I swallow and manage, 'You're going to play *rugby* with an *ostomy bag*?'

'That's the plan.'

'Wait, what? I didn't know you could do that!'

'Yeah. There's even a whole Rugby League team with ostomies. Quite a few professional sports people who've *had* ostomies too – usually temporary – because of Crohn's or ulcerative colitis: American footballers, baseball players, footballers, Olympians . . .

'Not sure if you know who Lewis Moody is, but he captained England rugby and was in the World Cup winning team. Turns out he had ulcerative colitis when he was playing! That kept me going when I was having a Crohn's flare in Fifth Form and the rugby coach wanted me to give up rugby. Lewis never got an ostomy though.'

'This is pickling my brain! I'm sure my stoma nurse told me the only thing I *can't* do with my bag is contact sports. What happens if you get a boot in your stoma?'

'Did your stoma nurse tell you the story about the person who was kicked in theirs by a horse?'

I grimace. 'No, she likes to keep things positive.'

'Yeah, I don't fancy a hoof in the gut, or someone's boot studs! But there're stoma guards. Little plastic helmets to protect them from impact. And I'll maybe strap bubble wrap over my bag like the doc did my ribs when I popped them, to stop someone ripping my bag clean off.'

My brain is exploding at this revelation. Implications on what this means for me. A re-evaluation of the fact that I've been blocking out the pain of not being able to play hockey. How I feel about myself. Who I am. Not just a weakling, sick Shit Bag . . .

A clear visual of Chris playing rugby next season settles in my mind's eye. And it fuels the dark side of my sense of humour. 'Tell you what,' I say. 'I'll make sure I'm watching next season when you play Lowettsons. But you have to do me a favour.'

'What's that?'

'Don't strap up your bag too tight. And don't empty it before you play.'

'Why?'

'Because I want you to dump a full bag of poo on Meathead's head. Wouldn't mind him getting called Shit Head . . .'

Chris gapes, but he's smiling at least. And says, 'Big guy? Second Row? Lumbering?'

'That's the one. He spread my Shit Bag nickname round school.'

Chris sucks air in through his teeth. 'Just for you, Shit Bag. I'll shit on his head.'

We high-five.

I press on my bag through my T-shirt to check it's still there and, looking at my scrawny bicep, I say, 'Have you started doing any training since you got your bag?'

Chris laughs and gestures to his body. 'Do I not look like I'm exercising?'

'Sorry, I didn't—'

'You're fine, Shit Bag. I had keyhole surgery so getting my bag wasn't that invasive. But it was a bad Crohn's flare that caused my bowel surgery. And I still have Crohn's in my remaining gut. It affects other parts of my body too – joints and skin, stuff like that. That's partly what delayed my return to weights and training.'

I nod, trying to take in everything he's telling me. 'Cody. She said she takes pred . . . something?' I can't remember what she said.

'Prednisolone. Yeah, I took that for a while. Doesn't work for me now. I'm on other stuff.' He picks up a pebble – someone must have collected it and others from the loch beach and lined them up on the step. Chris slings the stone at a nearby bin. It clatters on contact.

'What year are you in at Merchants?'

'I'm repeating – so I'm going back into Lower Six. Bit grim having to be in the same class as kids a year younger than me. While my mates are going to be taking their A levels.'

'You'll be in my year then.'

He looks at me and smiles. 'I will.'

'What subjects are you doing?' I ask.

'Biology, maths and chemistry.'

I nod. Another science boy – like Lockie. I wonder what Lockie would think if he knew I was here with Chris. He probably knows who Chris is from rugby. Maybe I'll post a photo of us *together*. That would cause a riot. Bet Lockie would rapidly materialise in my DMs too.

Chris is fiddling with the plastic bit on the end of his lace. He has those sculpted hands that natural athletes have. I track a raised vein with my eyes from the back of his hand up his forearm until it disappears out of sight on the inside of his elbow. He's been doing some weights then. The phlebotomists wouldn't have had trouble taking bloods or getting a line in him at least. Apparently I have narrow veins. Now collapsed narrow veins. There are still faint yellow marks on the backs of my hands left over from the black bruises when they had to keep relocating the cannula. 'What about you?' he says. 'What A levels are *you* doing?'

I flinch. 'I still have to sit three GCSEs. I missed them

because of hospital. But hopefully art, maths, history and physics at A level.'

'Interesting mix. And four! Do you know what you want to do at uni?'

'Yeah.'

'Is it a secret?'

'No . . . I just . . . if I can get that far, I'd like to do architecture – if I can get through the exams.' I focus on crushing the juice out of a dandelion flower. 'My concentration's shot since my surgery,' I admit. 'And I didn't do as well in my GCSEs as I wanted – I don't deal that well with stress. Did they blame stress when you had your big flare of Crohn's?'

'It can contribute. But it's genetics as well. And with my sport – I was probably pushing my body to its physical limits, eating a load of pizza and crap, and the stress of competing . . . None of that's really conducive to good things going on in your gut. I'd had food poisoning earlier in the year too though. Who knows!'

We sit for a moment in silence, and I watch a swan out on the loch dunk its head underwater for longer than I thought it'd be able to.

'Come on, Shit Bag.' Chris stands stiffly and offers me his hand. 'Let's get some lunch.'

I slide my hand inside his and he pulls me to my feet.

CHAPTER 16

We're all in the common room in our groups, for our afternoon psychological workshop.

'Fears!' Cody announces, lifting her thin brows. 'We're to say what makes us afraid.'

I use the distraction of Mel coming in late to the session – looking grim – to avoid catching Cody's eye, and volunteering myself to start. The last thing I need is to speak my dark thoughts into the air. Outwardly admit, and potentially bring into existence, that I don't know who I am anymore. I've lost my identity. As well as Lockie. That I don't know where I fit in my friend group now. Lockie and me were a team. And with that I had the friendship of Meathead and Shawsie. Or so I thought. Until I saw the Shit Bag meme and Suriya told me Lockie started it. I don't really understand what I've done so wrong for Meathead et al. to hate me so viciously that they'd spread that. Kick me when I'm already down. It's easy to joke about Chris emptying his bag on Meathead's head. But the reality of returning to school with my own bag, and nickname, has me terrified.

Mel's dragging a chair over the carpet tiles towards us. She thumps it down beside Chris and, legs crossed and folded up off the ground, demands in a more upbeat tone than her previous expression predicted, 'Where did you get to earlier?'

Chris makes eye contact with me. 'Nowhere.'

We all sit in silence. Looking at Mel.

'What?' she says.

'We're supposed to be doing the team exercise,' Chris says.

'Carry on then,' she says. 'What's the first question?'

'We're to share our fears,' Cody explains.

Mel shakes her head and rolls her eyes sky high. 'You serious?'

'I'll go first,' Cody offers. 'I'm afraid of . . .' She blushes a deep, hot pink. 'Oh, I don't know . . .'

'Don't answer that shit if you don't feel comfortable, Cody,' Mel says abruptly.

This is unexpected. Is there trouble in the house of the stoma nurse?

'Maybe I'll give this one a miss,' Cody rushes breathily. 'If that's okay? I do feel grateful to have what I still have . . .'

Owen smiles reassuringly at Cody.

I find myself nodding along. I wonder if Cody fears ending up with a permanent ostomy like Chris has. They both have Crohn's. Owen too. Is she not answering to protect Chris's feelings?

Chris is obviously making the absolute best of his life, trying to play rugby again. But if my assumption has crossed Chris's mind too . . . then surely this workshop's a bad thing for *his* confidence.

'I'm vetoing answering this question,' Mel says. 'My bloody mother hasn't got a clue!'

Woah. Okay . . . Things definitely aren't so tickety-boo with Judgy Long Legs and Mummy.

Cody reads the piece of paper. 'It says we don't have to answer out loud. Just it might be helpful to think about it.'

Mel says, 'Yeah, well, that's ableist bull excrement if ever I heard it. If you guys are anything like me, you've got a million fears firing through your head every day. They change. And isn't our biggest fear that we end up dying from this?' She points, with both index fingers like guns, to her stomach.

That's kind of heavy coming from the girl who's supposed to be fixed because she's got a pouch now!

'Oh, Mel!' Cody's voice breaks. And I realise she's welled up with tears.

'Cody, it's okay . . .' Chris says gently. 'Mel.'

Mel doesn't skip a beat. 'Let it out, Cody. This is what they want from us. Our *supportive* parents!'

'Mel, you're not helping,' Chris says calmly but with a stony tone.

'It is though. They want us all to cry and have deep and meaningful heartfelt conversations, and then come out the other side saying we're transformed and we're all better emotionally thanks to their clever questions. Go on, Cody, what's the next one?'

Aside from the uneasy feeling I'm starting to get about Mel's situation, she has a point.

Chris reaches out and Cody hands him the pieces of paper. He reads. Then says, 'What makes you happy?'

Mel snorts.

Chris's lips quirk into the hint of a smile.

'She's nothing if not consistent,' Mel says. '*I bet all the other parents would like their child to be happier and more upbeat about their lot too. I know! I'll get them all to say what makes them happy and then they'll automatically be much happier just thinking about it! I'm a genius!*'

Even though I've only heard it once, I instantly recognise Mel's uncanny impression of her mum's voice. She's kind of funny, this girl.

'What makes you happy, Cody?' Mel says.

Cody wipes her eyes. 'Uh, I don't know.'

'Sure you do. What's the thing that cheers you right up when you're feeling down?'

'Chocolate!' Cody brightens. 'I'm not supposed to eat it at the moment, but I sneak it when Mum isn't around.'

Owen answers KFC and rugby.

Chris smiles sadly. It occurs to me that his fear and happiness are probably wrapped up in that odd-shaped-ball package. He turns to Mel and stares at her, like he's saying, '*And you?*'

Mel pouts, thinking. And then passes on the baton again. 'Freya? What makes you happy?'

I find myself staring at her, blinking. I shrug. 'I don't know . . .' And look away from her to Chris. Honestly, I don't. Nothing feels exciting anymore. Nothing makes me happy. I feel nothing. Well, not happy things. I feel angry. I feel numb some days. I feel lonely. I . . . I miss my old life.

And suddenly I see it across the circle in Chris's blue-green eyes. A glassing-over like he knows. Like he's feeling the sickly pain in my chest. He understands. I blink quickly and look down to see my folded arms, hugging myself. 'Sorry,' I say. 'I can't really think . . .'

'Break!' Mel shouts, scaring me senseless. 'Break time, everyone!'

The noise across the room rumbles up like a kettle coming to the boil. And everyone around stretches and yawns, shakes off their tension.

I lock eyes with Chris, my lips still pinched tight. I'm stressed. Mel's right. This wasn't a good activity for me. Or any of us. Chris rubs the back of his neck.

'Let's have a pool tournament or table tennis or something to unwind,' Mel announces.

'Yeah. I'm up for that,' Chris says.

'Won't your mum be cross if we don't finish the activity?' Cody asks.

'She told everyone at induction they'd leave here feeling more confident about themselves. Do you feel more confident right now, Cody?'

Cody bites her lip. And then she surprises me by saying decisively, 'I'd like to go home more confident! I'd like to be able to speak up for myself. And make decisions . . . about my body.' Her smile widens when Owen grins at her.

Mel starts clapping in approval, slowly and purposefully. Chris joins in and Owen and I follow, upping the tempo. And the other teams, although they haven't a clue why they're doing it, clap too, whooping and cheering. Mel points and nods at Owen, and he shouts, 'I want to leave here with new friends and . . . Cody, will you come for a walk with me later?'

Everyone descends into a chaotic clash of screaming and whistling. Chris and I are laughing and clapping our hearts out. Cody's blushing beetroot but nodding wholeheartedly. She's so sweet and young-looking I keep forgetting that she's only a year younger than me.

Mel swings her arm to Chris. He grimaces but it morphs before my eyes into one of those huge grins he's so good at. The other teams have got the gist of what we're doing and the noise drops a couple of decibels.

'I want to leave here,' he shouts, 'able to do a backflip again!'

What? WHAT? That's the weirdest and most wasted wish for achievement EVER!

Mel screws up her nose that he wasted his magical wish. The genie in the lamp would have no trouble fulfilling that one. She takes a bow, straightens up and shouts, 'I want to leave here with my guts settled and being able to go for a jog without shitting my pants!'

Everyone shouts and screams and laughs at this, clapping and whooping even harder.

Except me.

I'm clapping with a strained mannequin smile.

What does she mean 'guts settled and not shitting her pants'? She's *fixed*. She has the pouch! Is this some kind of fucked-up joke?

She's pointing at me challenging me: *Make it a good one, roomie!*

And – I don't. All I can do is shake my head and

point to the next girl. Hoping *she* still harbours hopes and dreams.

By the time we've maxed out the positivity in the room, it's time for afternoon tea. Sounds quaint but this is another foible of an outward-bound activity camp with kids who aren't in peak physical condition. We're already a bit undernourished and then they're pushing us physically, so we need refuelling regularly.

We're all in the canteen loading up with sandwiches, crisps, Victoria sponge cake, and tea, juice or – if you really need building up – a fortified high-calorie milkshake.

'You guys okay?' Chris says, slumping into the chair beside me.

'Yeah, good,' I reply, turning my phone face down. I've been flicking through a guy from the rugby squad's recently uploaded pics, while Cody and Owen sit beside me, flirting. There must've been a beach party in Portugal last night. Weirdly, Morven and Suriya haven't posted any photos yet. Morven didn't mention it in her text either. '*You* okay?' I say.

'Great,' Chris says.

'Where's Mel gone?'

'Toilet.'

I nod. 'She okay?'

Chris pulls one of those fake smiles where you don't show your teeth and your eyebrows are up high. 'Yeah. Think she's good.'

I can't work out whether there's *a thing* going on between Chris and Mel or if I'm missing something bigger. I don't really know anything about her to be able to judge it. 'Mel suggested a pool or ping-pong tournament earlier, didn't she?' I say conversationally. 'Do you guys fancy playing tonight? If you don't have *other* plans.' I flick my head to Cody and Owen, meaning – if you and Mel aren't going for a *walk* like those two.

But before I can get a response from Chris, little Jessica muscles her way in between us, slurping her bottle of fortified milkshake through a straw. She elbows me and pauses her slurp to say, 'We're ready to decorate Henry's ostomy bag now.'

'Hi, Jessica, Henners,' I say. As usual, wee Henners is there hanging in Jessica's wake. 'I'm well, thank you. Thanks for asking. How are you this fine afternoon?'

Jessica regards me steely-eyed over the top of the bottle and sucks again.

'Yeah, okay, just let me finish my food first,' I concede. 'Then we'll get some pens.'

She nods and wanders away with Henners trailing her.

'I think she likes you,' Chris says.

I smile. 'Is that what that is?'

'Heya!' Mel materialises and slides in on the seat beside Chris. She rubs the green apple she's carrying on his sleeve and takes a bite. 'What's up?'

'We're planning a ping-pong tournament,' Chris says. 'What're your thoughts?'

'Yeah. We've five nights left. Is that enough time?'

'If we play doubles, sure,' Chris says, smiling at me.

Mel sees it and looks me up and down briefly, before saying to Chris, 'Fine. But you're playing on my backhand side.'

Great. Who can *I* play with?

Mel and Chris are chatting about someone I don't know who's back in hospital. So I lift my phone again and do my best to zone out. Someone touches my arm and I jump at the contact. It's Cody. 'Would you like another piece of cake? I got too much,' she says, smiling.

'Umm, okay,' I say, looking back at my phone. I glance to Cody. She's biting her lip.

I set my phone down before me. 'Diet Coke!' I blurt. 'I really like Diet Coke. Like you love chocolate.'

'Diet Coke.' Cody beams.

'Though I can't drink it anymore.' I look down morosely at my phone and something white in the picture, behind Shawsie and Meathead wrestling on the beach, catches my eye.

'Why not?' Cody says.

Looks like Suriya – that's her white ASOS dress. The one she got for her mum and dad's wedding anniversary party.

'Fizzy drinks can make our bags blow up with air,' Chris answers for me. I hadn't realised he was listening.

Wait. That's Suriya lying on . . . Looks like . . . Can't – hot flush. Can't – *neeagh* – no. No. Zoomed in. Eye close. White lace dress. Hand. Thigh. Purple *Supreme* T-shirt. Tongue. Throat. LOCKIE. Hypervent – *Retch*.

'Not again,' Cody sobs.

'Have some water.'

'*Nggaa! Ngga. Gah.*'

'Freya. Deep breaths. Owen, get a basin from the kitchen.'

'That,' I pant for air, 'BI-TCH!'

CHAPTER 17

I sit rocking on my bed in my cell, staring at the message I've just sent Morven:

> **Me:** I know! Tell Suriya – I never want to speak to her again.

I'm running out of loose bits of skin around my nails to chew on while I wait for Morven's response.

I found another picture online, with them in the background. Suriya sitting between Lockie's legs, his arms around her waist, lips on her neck.

I hear a high-pitched whining-squeal sound from Mel's side of the room. And Mel, who's sat with me while I've raged hellfire and turned the air thick and blue, instantly drops her legs off the side of her bed and plants her hands on her thighs.

She brought me here. Told me to hold it together. Reminded me that there were little kids – Jessica and Henners – around. Parents too. Told me I could swear and scream all I wanted once we were in here. That she'd scream and swear at anyone I wanted her to. As long as I held my composure until we were in private.

'I have to go to the toilet—! You okay on your own?' Mel says quickly. 'I can get Chris.'

My phone rings with a new video-call from Morven.

I stare at it.

It stops ringing pretty quickly, Mel's already at the door. She waves briefly and rushes out into the hall.

I inhale and force air from my lungs. I rub my face and let out a feral growl, 'Uuugghhh!'

My phone rings again.

I repeat the inhale-exhale and answer it. I see Morven's worried expression on my phone and my pulse drums in my throat. 'Is Suriya there?' I say.

'Yes, do you want—'

'No! Tell her to piss off.'

Morven looks over the top of her screen. She widens her eyes and then clicks her tongue. 'Wait a minute . . .' She carries me through white corridors outside so that I can see a deep-blue sky above her. 'I'm so sorry, honey.'

'Are they together?'

Morven bites her bottom lip in response.

128

'Oh my God. What? After one night? I'm going to be sick.'

'It's not just one night . . .'

An industrial rubbish compactor is crushing my body. I close my eyes, desperate not to let tears free.

'It's just – we didn't – you've been so . . . ill.'

I open my eyes.

'And you missed . . . I didn't want to hurt you any more, Frey. Suriya promised me . . .' As Morven looks at me, a tear trails slowly down each of her cheeks. *Pity tears.*

I scrub away mine and wipe my nose with the back of my hand. 'When? When did they—' Guh. I want to . . . Guh. 'First?'

'My pool party. After the end-of-term ball.'

I can't even speak.

That was the same night Suriya sat in my hospital room and told me Lockie started my Shit Bag nickname.

That the boys thought he was lucky to be rid of me, now I had my disgusting bag. That he'd laughed at me.

She even promised she'd give Lockie a piece of her mind! That she had my back.

'But I didn't know until Marbella!' Morven says. 'She only admitted it then. They've been sneaking around. Up until last night hardly anyone knew but Meathead got this bottle of fruit brandy and they got pissed . . .'

Morven's known since Marbella. I clamp my lips. Partly

to stop myself from puking and partly to stop myself from telling Morven I never want to speak to *her* ever again. I turn it into a grimace, nod and say, 'I need to go.'

'Frey—!'

'I've got to—' I kill the connection. And immediately yank Morven's silver friendship bracelet – aka Marbella guilt-gift – off my wrist, throw it across the room, scream and burst into breathless, angry, blubbering tears.

I'm swiping through photos comparing myself to Suriya when there's a knock on the cell door and Mel sticks her head around it. 'Are we good to come in?'

'Look at this!' I say, holding up my phone and jabbing at the screen. 'Look at her. No wonder he's with her! And look at this one—' I swipe again and push my phone out into the air so Mel can get an eyeful of my ex-best-friend in '*that white bikini*' she wore to Morven's pool party. 'See her stomach!'

Mel steps forward, and after a brief glance and quirk of her eyebrows, she says, 'It's very stomachy . . .'

I glare at her. 'Thanks. Easy for you to make jokes about. Now you've got your pouch. Maybe try remembering what it's like having a bag of shit stuck there all day, every day. Disgusting! That's what they all think of me. Foul. Stinking. Ugly. Rank! If I don't get rid of this *thing*, I may as well DIE!'

Mel turns away, saying, 'Chris!' as the cell door clicks closed in its frame. She swings round on me, snapping, 'You know *nothing* about what I'm going through! Or anyone else here! You're so caught up being the only *victim*. I don't give a shit if some random boy fancies your *friend* more than you. With your attitude, I don't blame him. Your friend's fit! Get over it.

'All I care about right now is *my* friend just heard you spouting shite about wanting to die if you don't get rid of your bag. When his bag is permanent!'

And she slams the door after her.

I sit stunned. I hadn't realised Chris was standing right behind her.

I text Mum and Dad to tell them I'm really tired and I don't want to video-call tonight. Annabelle appears a little while later – she checks I'm happy with my bag – and says she'll bring me a tray with dinner so I can have a quiet night to myself. I desperately want to apologise to Chris. But I physically can't bring myself to leave this cell, other than to rush along to the loos during dinner to empty my bag while the corridor is clear.

I hear lots of people screaming and laughing, shouting to each other, as the night progresses. And every time a voice looms near I hold my breath. In case it's Mel. Cody.

Chris. Someone, coming to see me. To get me to join the ping-pong tournament. But they don't. So I hide under the horrible synthetic duvet, looking at ancient photos of me and Lockie that I've retrieved from the iCloud's back-up files, and cry.

CHAPTER 18

I pretend I'm asleep when Mel slips into the cell at ten forty-five. I pretend not to wake when she goes to the loo at three a.m. And again at five twenty-three a.m. By now I'm desperate for the loo myself, my bag is so inflated it's in danger of lifting me off the mattress like a hot-air balloon. But I don't want Mel to know I'm awake, so I lie like a plank for another half-hour after she gets back into bed, listening for her breathing shift, and then I slip out into the hall and stumble along to the loo.

I empty the air from my balloon, clean the end and close the clip. My tummy gurgles. Now that the air pressure is released, my stoma will probably move any moment, so I lean my head against the side of the cubicle and have a little snooze. I don't know how long I've dozed off, but I'm woken by another cubicle door slamming. I quickly empty my bag again, clean and clip it, and flush. I smack the hand-dryer again on the way out and mooch back to the room. But just before I push into my cell, I hear a door click open and a hinge squeak. I look back along the corridor. A dark neck, buzzed hair and navy-blue training gear are quickly replaced by the swinging fire door.

Where's Chris going at six a.m.?

I need to apologise.

So I follow him. Along the corridor, through the fire door, past the reception desk and outside. The early morning sun is hitting the lodge – I'm blinded by its brilliance. I squint and make out Chris walking down the path towards the playground. He has his arm crooked with something pink tucked under his elbow and his shoulders hunched. It's at this moment I remember I'm in my slippers and pyjamas, braless. He stops at the swings and props what I recognise now as a pink gym-shaker-bottle and another orange bottle against one of the uprights. He sucks from a foil packet and sets that down too.

He puts both arms above his head as if he's hailing the sun, points them and then bends forward and touches his hands on the ground, and then he's down into a lunge . . . and a plank. He's doing yoga! I don't want him to see me, but I can't go back inside. I have to watch. Like I'm some sort of pervert. A yoga fetishist. This guy is doing yoga in such a legit, serious way that I can't miss it. I creep back up the path and skirt along the front of the left bothy annexe, sitting down in the warmth of the sun, against the wall, and watch Chris. He stretches through his yoga routine three times and then stands and loosens his shoulders. He holds onto the upright of the swing for balance and pendulums his leg back and forth. Does it for the other. Then lies down. Throws his straight right leg over the left, bending at the hip to stretch out his lower back. He's thorough with his stretches. I bet the Lowettsons rugby boys in Portugal are nowhere near as thorough as this.

Next, push-ups. Slow at first then fast power push-ups. I had no idea that was possible with a bag. Although, he said he had keyhole surgery so maybe they didn't cut through his abs like they did mine. Then he does pull-ups on the swings' crossbar. I count fifty-six before he abruptly drops back to the ground and holds his stomach like he's got a stitch. He yanks up his training top, catches it with his chin and I see a black, rigid belt wrapped around his brown stomach. He pulls it off easily as if it's fastened with Velcro and I see his bag. It's similar to mine in shape but Chris's bag doesn't match his skin colour. His is grey. But most striking of all, I realise, is Chris doesn't have the big scar I have! So keyhole surgery means no scar? None that I can see from here, anyway. Leaving me admiring the view of his exposed half-grid pattern of defined, lean abs.

Oddly, an image of our differing stomachs combines in

my mind, conjuring a symbolic noughts-and-crosses cum snakes-and-ladders game: his grid, our stomas and my jagged ladder of stapled stiches. I bury my smile in the sleeve of my pyjama top.

Chris prods down the side of his bag as if he's feeling for something, and jumps when he pokes a sore spot. He tips his head back, having a moment, the sun on his face. I bite at my thumb, wanting to go and see if he's okay. But he looks down again, resolute, and wraps the thick belt – it must be elasticated – tight around his stomach. He steps up unsteadily onto the swing again and, more slowly this time, pulls himself up on the crossbar for seven more chin-ups. He picks up his pink bottle, takes a swig, sets it down again, lifts the orange and the foil packet, which I guess must be one of those glucose gel packs we use during hockey matches, and runs away from the playground down towards the loch.

I sit in the sun and think about yesterday. What I said. Chris is trying to make the best of his situation and planning on getting back in Merchants Firsts. Something verging on the impossible? And here's me crying and screaming because my ex has pulled my friend, because she's got a pretty tummy and no shit bag. And mentally abusing Chris while I'm at it. And after he helped me change my bag. He could've just sent Annabelle or even Mel to rescue me. Mel, who would've screamed at me and told me to *grow up and slap a new flange on!* Easy for her to say when she doesn't have one. But still, she's supportive of Chris. So why can't I be? When I'm still living with my ostomy.

Maybe Mel's right. Everyone here has their own shit going on and it's my turn to give someone else support back.

I wait until I can see Chris returning, jogging along the pebbly edge of the beach, and I walk down the path to meet him.

He stops, air grating out of his throat, and leans on his knees. He spits to the side. I wave a window-wiper hello and wait until he recovers enough to not sound like he's about to expire. He sits on the grass, and I join him – remembering a tad late that I'm still in my pyjamas.

Now I'm sat, I say quickly, 'I'm really sorry about yesterday. I didn't know you were there. But that shouldn't matter. Saying things like . . . what I said. It's obviously bullshit. I wouldn't want to . . . die. I was just being dramatic. And self-centred . . .'

'Did Mel tell you to say that?' he says all monotone, between breaths.

Eyeing him, to gauge whether there's a chink in his emotional armour, I say, 'No. I thought that up all by myself.'

Chris nods. 'Okay. I'm sorry your boyfriend can't keep it in his pants.'

I gasp at his savagery. 'He's my ex, actually.'

'And what? You still want him back?'

'No . . .' Probably. 'It's not just him though. Suriya's one of my best friends. And my other bestie knew and didn't tell me! There's supposed to be a girl code.'

'You know there's a boy code too, right? Don't pull your ex's best friend is at least number three in the manual.'

'What's number one and two, dare I ask?'

Chris quirks a smile and taps his nose. 'Secret.'

'Hmm, I'm not sure Lowettsons boys are working to the same manual as Merchants.'

'You're hanging out with the wrong school's boys then.'

'Maybe I am . . .'

Chris waves his hand loosely. 'Honestly, my view's pretty simple. If someone cheats on you or acts like they don't respect you, then you need to recognise what they're showing you and cut them loose.'

I feel reprimanded. Guilty as charged. 'Okay,' I say, almost whispering.

'Not you, numpty. I mean in a relationship.'

'So you know I didn't mean what I said about the bag? You forgive me?'

'I'll give you the benefit of the doubt.'

Suddenly realising how totally weird that saying is, I say,

'What does that phrase actually mean – the benefit of the doubt?'

Chris sighs. 'Who knows, Shit Bag! Your brain's way too alert for this time in the morning.' And he reaches out and ruffles my hair with long, athletic fingers, like I'm a cute puppy.

And for once, I kinda feel cute too.

CHAPTER 19

During breakfast – a frosty affair thanks to Mel still freezing me out (who knows why *she's* consistently more offended by my 'disrespect' towards ostomates than anyone who actually has a bag) – we're reminded to wear swimwear under our clothes ready for today's physical activity: canyoning.

'What's canyoning?' I say to Chris.

'You go up a mountain and slide down rivers and rock pools in a wetsuit and abseil down rock faces.'

'You're joking?'

He beams and shakes his head. 'We're pushing ourselves beyond our physical comfort zone, remember. And it's fun!'

And I can't help myself. 'Not being rude, Mel, but considering your mum's a stoma nurse you'd think she'd know our limitations. How many loos are on this mountain exactly?'

Mel bumps the table – clattering the breakfast crockery – as she scrapes her chair back, and speed-walks out of the canteen.

I side-eye Chris, waiting for him to either tell me off or elaborate on why Mel's so flipping sensitive but he just cuts into his bacon and poached eggs on toast and forks some into his mouth.

'And abseiling, you say?' I turn to him. 'They know my scar's not totally sound! And now I think about it – didn't you hurt yourself doing all those pull-ups this morning at the swings?'

Chris wipes his mouth and doesn't meet my eye. 'I didn't hurt myself.'

'Yeah, you did, you—' I decide to finish my toast and shut up. If he's not admitting he's hurt himself then it's none of my business. And anyway, I don't have a swimming costume with me, so I probably won't have to go canyoning. Because why would I bring a swimming costume to a campsite in Scotland when I had my guts cut out barely two months ago? Flashing my now bumpy silhouette to all around is not something I want to be doing, even at Camp Kill Me All Over Again.

Yeah, so Mum packed my swimsuit.

And Beverley and Annabelle – the Plotting Stoma Nurse

Pair – checked with my surgeon before camp so I'm good to go canyoning. Whoop de doo.

I'm waiting on the bus with Cody and Owen when Mel climbs on board, changed from what she was wearing earlier – she's in a crop top, looking all tall, willowy and just a bit model-esque and then I realise as she walks towards me that *I can see her stoma scar*. She's not hiding it. She has low-slung jeans on and she's just showing off her scar. Not that it even looks like a scar, more like a greying bruise, which is probably why it took me a moment to remember that she used to have a stoma there.

She's watching me, so I have to look away. But I desperately want to stare at the little mark. To see what I'll have after my reversal. After my gut sausage pieces are sewn back together and pushed back inside so my intestine can get on with doing its job in private.

Oh, to have my innards private again!

And here comes Chris behind. And Mel turns her back on me and says to him, 'Can you take the window? I'll get car sick otherwise.' She's body-blocking me. Chris is *her* friend not mine. Message received, loud and clear.

But I can see the side of her tummy from here. If I just lean back against the window and pull my feet up onto the seat and get out my phone and pretend I'm looking through photos.

It's a slight indent to the right of her belly button,

greyish-brown – it really is like a bruise. She could probably get a tattoo over that if she wanted and no one would ever know she's had her large intestine removed. I've seen uglier appendix scars at school.

But then she hitches up her waistband as they're talking, like she knows I'm watching, and I can't see the scar at all anymore. She's just a girl sitting beside a boy on a bus, chatting and laughing and living her life.

I distract myself from their easy conversation and really do look through my phone for more photos of Portugal. After my chat with Chris, I've been thinking about the whole Lockie and Suriya thing. How that's come about. And how I feel – beyond my knee-jerk reaction of wishing plague and pestilence upon them.

I know Lockie couldn't handle the sight of my bag.

That second time he visited the hospital with his mum and dad, he wouldn't come near me. He sat mute instead, on the edge of the slippery, plasticated recliner by the door, like he was hoping its surface would facilitate a quick and fluid exit from my sick den, back to fresh air and freedom.

He wasn't even going to kiss me goodbye.

Ems had to order him, when they were already out in the corridor, to 'go back and hug Freya goodbye, Lochlan!' And in he came, shifty-eyed, offering a brief one shoulder and arm with an awkward pat.

'Bye. Take care.'

Just imagine how that hurts. When you're at your lowest. Broken into bits. *Cut* into bits! That's all you get from the boy you lost your virginity to!

So forgive me for my fixation with getting rid of this bag. The only way to do that is to get the pouch operation like Mel. Leaving all the other ostomates and Chris with his permanent bag behind.

I know I'll never be like Mel completely. She doesn't have my long zipper scar from crotch to stomach. But if there's a chance of me re-entering the world and competing against Suriya of the Unadulterated Belly Skin, then I'll take it. Like I said to Morven, I can always get a tattoo. I'll just be an edgier version of Mel. Let's see who Lockie likes best then, Suriya!

Tired after my second night of broken sleep, I lean against the window and watch the rain-spattered undergrowth along the roadside for a while as the bus winds through the trees. I can't wait to get home to my own bed. I nod off.

But then my mobile vibrates in my hand and I'm pulled back to life. It's Morven:

Morven: Thinking of you always! Miss you! Wish you were here with us!

144

Accompanied by a selfie in her yellow-and-pink training gear displaying the white block-caps RB on her hockey bib. An AstroTurf pitch in the background. Sure, Morven. You're always thinking of me, while you watch Lockie and Suriya eat face. And wishing I was there to what? Watch them too?

This sets me into a foot-wiggling, arm-crossing, body-hugging, thumbnail-biting agitation. Thanks for reminding me, *bestie*.

And suddenly I have the sensation of my stomach plummeting through my pelvis. I swipe through the photos of Suriya that I fixated on yesterday. And here it is.

I was too preoccupied to register what she was wearing over her hockey polo shirt. Probably because I'm so used to seeing it when I pull the bib on during training.

IL – for Inside Left.

Not only has Suriya taken my man, she's taken my hockey position too!

CHAPTER 20

At the activity centre, they size us up for wetsuits and herd all the girls into the locker room, to change first.

I'm so glad I wore a long, loose T-shirt over my turquoise swimming costume because despite the costume's roominess now I'm working the emaciated look, the Lycra's still accentuating my stoma like I'm smuggling a gobstopper on my abdomen. I manage to get the wetsuit up onto my hips. My thighs aren't creating much resistance these days. I have a thigh abyss rather than a gap. Who knew a girl would miss having thighs-she-could-crush-a-watermelon-with! Yeah, okay. I haven't tried that, but maybe someday in my future I'll go by Melon Crusher instead of Shit Bag.

'Could you zip me up, Freya?' Cody says, turning her back to me.

'For sure,' I say, pulling together the two sides of her overstretched suit. Hmm, I think they should've given

Cody a size up, but I wouldn't dare say that. Chris explained to me that the reason she has such a puffy face is because the drugs she's on are anti-inflammatory steroids, which seems bizarrely incongruous with the physical side effects they're manifesting. Because poor Cody looks inflated. Like those sailor boy marshmallows in *Ghostbusters*. So I just try my best to pull at the neoprene and join it. And as I do so, I see the marks on her skin, across her spine. Like horizontally stacked punctuation long-dashes of thinned, stretched skin.

'Just watch out for my stretch marks,' she says, like she's reading my mind. 'If that's okay.'

'Course,' I say quickly, feeling stupid that I didn't even know you could get stretch marks like that as a teen. I mean, not being rude but Cody isn't *big* big. She's just puffy. But no matter how much I try, my stupid fingers can't get the zip together.

Not knowing what to do, I say pathetically, 'Mel?'

Mel laser-glares me for interrupting her while she's helping one of the other girls pull up a neoprene leg. She's crouched and flexed in this tiny bikini, like she's the ultimate surfer girl, with a stoma scar bruise. But she sees my wide eyes of panic and says, 'Cody, if you end up needing the toilet you won't be able to get that off quickly enough. Give me a sec and I'll get you a better wetsuit. They've given me a crap one too.'

And with a few quick moves, Mel's sorted out the other girl, checked the size on Cody's suit and walked out into the wide open in her bikini.

I sit down on the locker-room bench, feeling drained by my exertions and with renewed envy towards Mel.

I want to be her.

I want to be at that stage in my journey.

If I get there, I'll be the happiest person in the entire world. I know I will.

That sounds idealistic. Or is it being a realist? Expecting something so basic as getting rid of an ostomy bag? Sold to me by the surgeon, stoma nurse and my parents as something I can return. Give it back when it's the right time. Surely that's realistic? Not asking that much!

I zip my wetsuit up enough that the protruding outline of my stoma is covered, then I pull my T-shirt up over my head. How am I going to change at school with all this to cover up? At least here, a bag isn't that abnormal.

I look round the room trying to stocktake on who else has a bag and I finally spot little Jess over by the door rocking a rainbow-unicorn-and-stars repeat print one-piece costume. That girl's got the right amount of attitude. She squeals as her mum lifts her fully up off the ground as they try to pull the back of her wetsuit up. I realise that the busy pattern on her costume is so distracting that I'd never have guessed Jess has a colostomy under there. I look down at my own block-colour costume. I guess I'll have to go loud too if I want to go to Morven's next pool party.

I'm togged up in wetsuit, helmet and life jacket, standing outside the activity centre's sheds feeling slightly concerned by the general need for such safety equipment. I have way too many protruding bones that remain unprotected – like my shoulders and my hips and my coccyx . . . And also, the wetsuit's sort of dragging everything down around my bag area. Which doesn't feel that secure.

'Hey, Chris,' I say when I see him.

'When Annabelle said she'd push us out of our comfort zone,' he says, stretching his leg up as if he's warming up to do hurdles, 'I didn't realise they'd be vacuum-packing us.'

'Bit tight then?'

'Yeah!' He walks round the corner of the shed, shirks off his helmet and life jacket and struggles to catch the cord hanging from the zip at the back of his wetsuit. 'Can you unzip me?' he says.

'Sure.' I pull the zip down and he struggles out of the wetsuit's top. Until I'm faced with the bare concave dip of his lower back. I stare at it, wondering how I'm suddenly in this situation: standing behind a shed with Chris half unwrapped. And contemplate what might happen if I run my fingertips down his spine to see if he's ticklish. But obviously I don't, and instead step back to create a little space. Chris turns to face me as he shoves his fists in the front of the wetsuit as if he's trying to create a kangaroo pouch at the front for his bag. Which inevitably makes me want to look down at his crotch because wetsuits are like that, they act as crotch magnets for eyes. So I stare at his neck. Then his shoulder. Naked boy pec. Abs . . . And turn away. To inspect the wood grain of the shed.

'Ahh! That's better,' he sighs. And when I dare to look back, he's got his elbow contorted inside the shoulder part to stretch that section of the neoprene out too.

Once I've got him all zipped in again, he asks, 'Do you want me to do you now?'

I manage to squeak, 'Maybe later.'

CHAPTER 21

I'm feeling marginally more optimistic and upbeat about getting wet and wild this afternoon – with Chris, and the rest of my team. Then Mel's mum, Annabelle, pours icy water on my spirits.

'What do you mean, we're in the same team?' Mel says to her mum.

'After yesterday's to-do, it's clear you're not speaking to each other, so we've decided you and Freya should work it out together as a team,' Annabelle replies, tying a yellow tag of plastic ribbon to Mel's helmet so she matches me and Chris.

'What to-do?' Mel says indignantly.

'Everyone heard you screaming and yelling, Amelia! So go sort it out on the mountainside.'

'Fuck sake,' Mel says, walking away.

'I expect you girls to be friends by the time you're back here!'

So this feels like the perfect time to sum up today's fun, team-bonding activity of canyoning. You get togged up in rudimentary safety gear, wear your own trainers – mine were nice turquoise Asics. *Were*, because fifteen minutes in they'd turned the colour of the sludge water sloshing between my toes.

You get ferried in Land Rovers up into the heady heights of a local mountain. They unload you like a colony of defenceless seals to the slaughter, line you up, show you a river, aka nature's version of a slip-and-slide crossed with a mile-and-a-half-long rocky flume system.

Then they push you off.

And it's on you to get yourself and your teammates – regrouping at each stage for a yellow ribbon headcount before you can progress to the next stage of the descent – down to the bottom of said water course and mountain.

But we're not talking paths or roads. No. Instead, you just throw yourself down the river like you're a dislodged boulder. Smacking your helmet-head against rocks. Catching your way-too-bony hip bones and coccyx on any natural protrusion too hard to be worn smooth by the river or waterfalls.

Yeah, because there are waterfalls too.

And when you've had your stomach muscles cut, you can't really use the abseiling ropes they've laid over the edge for you to lower yourself in a controlled manner. Instead, you just let go and fall into the murky depths of an ice-cold mountain pool.

And if you're thirsty on the way down, you'd think you could just have a sip of that pure, glacial spring water *à la* Highland Spring's advertising.

They lied.

'Cause this mountain spring ain't pure as the driven snow (watch that yellow snow, people). No, this water is as pure as the decomposing sheep upstream. Whose detached head – literally, no joke – sailed over a waterfall like a converted rugby ball, closely accompanied by Mel Hammer-Horror-screaming that the skull – with horns, teeth and shredded pale-pinky-white flesh hanging like fake Halloween cobwebs – had jostled her for pole position all the way down the river before victoriously plopping into the water below, to bob up and down beside my face as I tried redundantly to pull myself up out of the pool onto the next stage of this hell-ride downhill.

'Lever your feet against the edge,' the guy from the activity centre suggests to me helpfully, as the other guy manages to hook the sheep skull to safety with a hook-on-a-pole like that bobbing rubber duck game.

'I can't!' I growl, letting go of the rope and glaring at my man. Could he not just hook *me* out? I kick back and gesture for Mel to feel free to make her way up the rope next. 'You can go first,' I say.

Mel swims forward. 'Why, thank you, Shit Bag, that's very considerate of you.'

'I thought so,' I say, and realise this is the first time Mel's used my nickname. Does this mean we're becoming friends? Is her mum's plan working? Only, I suspect Mel means shitbag in the contemptible-person way, rather than acknowledging my preferred nickname.

But then, just as Mel's halfway up the rope, casting shade on me, Owen makes his explosive entrance into our waterfall pool. And with that huge splash, I swallow a load of Eau de Dead Sheep mountain water. Choke. And end up half drowning through inhalation.

The two activity centre guys and Owen do indeed have to use the hook to haul me out of the pool like a limp, dead – but strangely resistant and insolent despite being deceased – slippery selkie.

While Mel chokes too, with laughter.

We're ensconced on a large rock formation waiting for Cody and Chris, when Mel snorts, 'That was hilarious, Shit Bag. You looked . . . pathetic!' She tucks her trainered feet up on the rock and grips her shins tightly, like she's squeezing the life out of herself. *Yeah, it wasn't that funny, love.* I hear a rumble from her stomach and she releases her legs. Stands up. Paces away and back again and sits back on the rock.

I blink, battling my irritation with Mel. But I don't want to pick another fight. She's calling me Shit Bag now, at least. If that's progress? And she was decent yesterday when I first saw that photo of Lockie and Suriya together. So I don't take the bait for once, and keep my mouth shut.

'I'm freezing,' she says after a moment. 'Are you freezing?'

'Yeah,' I say, as a warm flood spills into my bag. 'Oh! Nope! Not anymore.' I point to my stomach and prod the now-squidgy ballooning below my wetsuit. 'Bet you miss having a portable hot poo bottle on your tummy, don't you!' I laugh, all light, trying to sweeten her mood.

'Yeah, maybe I do,' she says tightly.

Back to dour and cold Mel it is then. It's not like I'm trying to do what your mum suggested and make friends, Mel. It's not like I apologised *already* to Chris about yesterday and he and me are good. I snap, 'Well, I miss being able to tuck my knees to my chest like you're doing right now!' I push myself off the rock and stand. 'And I miss wearing bikinis and crop tops, so aren't you lucky!' I go say bye to Rabbie the ram skull.

* * *

155

We get to the next big drop, over a wide flat rock into what the guides tell us is the last and deepest – and therefore the coldest – of the pools. And to top it off, they explain we're to smile on the way down because we're being filmed.

Our team teeter on the edge, looking down into the water.

'Ladies first,' Owen says.

I say to Mel, 'You can go first.'

'On the contrary, Shit Bag,' Mel says. 'It's your turn to go first.'

'No, I insist,' I say, trying – and failing – to think of something I can call Mel with equal sarcasm to my *Shit Bag*.

'No!' Mel says. '*I* insist.'

We simultaneously turn to Chris.

He shrugs. 'Chivalry and all that. One of you go first. Or let Cody.'

'Equal opportunities,' I say.

'Oh well . . .' Mel says reluctantly. 'If you insist!'

And suddenly my shoulder jars and I'm air-walking off the edge and into the frigid water below.

Surfacing, I gasp for breath, my brain catching up and remembering there's a camera somewhere. 'You absolute—!' But before I get to curse Mel, there's a scream and she drops fast, twisting ungracefully, to smack into the bobbing water like a squashed fly on a windscreen.

I look up to see Chris grinning over the edge and Cody gaping wide-eyed.

Mel surfaces gasping, 'Chris! You wait!'

'Move out of the way, please!' he shouts. And Mel and I kick frantically back to opposite edges of the rock pool, looking up.

Chris disappears from view and I kick further round, worried he's doing a run-up and will hit me when he lands. But instead, I suddenly see his feet where his head used to be and in one folding, tumbling movement he drops forward from his handstand to twist round in the air, controlled this time, and enters the water feet first like a hot knife through warm butter.

And across the barely there splash of displaced water, Mel and I make wide eye contact. And she grins.

CHAPTER 22

'I'm using it for my passport photo,' Mel says, as we walk along the corridor to our cell.

I respond, 'I'm using mine for my Tinder profile.'

Mel gasps.

I nod, smirking. Proud of that one. And push into the room.

'Wait, you have Tinder?' Mel says, following me.

'Well, no. But when I do, this'll be my photo to lure the hot boy-flesh in.' I wave my photo-still taken from the canyoning last-drop video in a come-hither way.

Mel laughs and looks at her photo. The staff at the activity centre thought our videos were so hysterical that they presented us with stills for no extra cost.

'Not sure I can top that,' Mel muses. 'Though Mum will probably use mine for our family Christmas card . . . ?'

I nod. 'Not bad. But—!' I dance side to side with my

photo theatrically. Because I've just thought of my best yet. 'I see *your* family Christmas card and I raise you – Photoshopping in a wedding dress and putting it among my wedding photos!' I jump back onto my mattress and remember, just before impact, how hard and bumpy the bed is. 'Oww!'

Mel collapses onto her bed laughing, and then winces immediately herself. I presume her mattress is like mine, but when I realise she's frozen still, I focus on her. She looks like she's fighting some sort of inner battle. And then her muscles relax. And I hear the loudest rumble of thunder, from her gut.

'You okay?' I say.

'Living the dream, Shit Bag! What was that you said earlier? I'm *the lucky one* . . . You have no idea!'

'Woah.' I put my hands up in surrender. 'I thought we were being friends. I meant that as a positive thing. You have everything I want.'

She shakes her head as if she's shaking off her mood, but she doesn't smile. 'I need you to stop saying I'm lucky.'

I shift carefully on my bed.

'I know you hate your bag, and you want rid of it ASAP. And maybe your pouch will be great for you! But that's not my experience right now. Things aren't great for me.'

I stare at her, my pulse drumming in my throat. 'Okay . . . ?'

She winces again, bracing herself rigid, then she relaxes. And there comes another roll of thunder from her belly.

'Do you need to go to the loo?'

'Yep. But it's temperamental. Sometimes I have to wait until I'm really desperate otherwise I'll have to keep going back.' She crosses her legs and arms tightly, hugging herself.

I go over to join her and sit on the end of her bed. I bite my bottom lip. 'Is it always like this?'

She shrugs and points to her stomach. 'This is nothing.'

I bite the skin beside my thumbnail. 'What else?'

'Lots. First, they said I had pouchitis. That's inflammation. But the antibiotics didn't help and instead they made me constipated so I couldn't go to the toilet without having to pummel my stomach with my fists. And then I could go but just a little. But when I'd stand and leave the toilet, I'd immediately need to go again, but I wouldn't be able.' She nods her head to the side. 'I tried super-strength probiotics. Lots of different ones. Did low FODMAP for a while.'

I squint my lips in pretend acknowledgement and then admit, 'What's a FODMAP?'

'Restrictive diet. Stands for fermentable oligo-some-sugar-shit, with a dose-of-more-sugar-shit, and mono-sugar-shit and poly-all-the-whatsits. Basically, reducing certain carbs that the small intestine can't absorb properly.'

'Right . . .'

'You asked!'

'I want to know. It's just, this doesn't totally compute. And you look so pulled together from the outside. I mean, you're fixed!'

'Me living in the toilets day and night hasn't given you a little hint that I'm not?'

I grimace. I noticed. But she's right. I didn't *notice*. I've been kind of caught up with my own *issues* as Mum would call it. Yeah, I'm a shitbag. 'Well, maybe if you share?' I shrug. 'Talking about your experiences might make you realise your pouch isn't *that* bad.'

'Oh, *maybe*,' she says, sounding super upbeat. 'What other *experiences* would you like to know about?'

I shrug. 'Everything.'

'Everything? Hmm, let me see . . .' Mel says, tapping her finger on her chin. 'So you want to know that my guts are always cramping and the only way to *not* shit myself is if I freeze and don't move a muscle until the spasm subsides? But then soon as I'm over that pain, my gut embarrasses me by immediately growling at everyone in a mile radius? Is that the sort of experiences you wanted me to share?' *Oh! Not upbeat. Sounding sarky now.* 'And because this happens *all* the time, I know when it's coming so I have to do this fucked-up dance of freezing but then grab a pillow or a jumper or fold my arms or speak loudly or shift around loudly to try and muffle that growling noise? How's that?'

I grimace. *That sounds not that great . . .*

'And my guts are never normal. Both our colons are gone, remember! The poo's never solid. I wear pant liners every day! Just in case. On a bad day you'll be shitting water. And that'll be because you ate a piece of fruit. Or you drank some coffee. Or it happens to be a day ending in Y. You know sphincters aren't designed to keep in water, right?'

This sounds worryingly familiar. 'Surely you can do everyday stuff though? You said you wanted to go for a jog. That was an exaggeration. You *can* go for a jog, right?'

'As long as I don't eat beforehand and I take a bucket-load of loperamide, then I can go for a run or go down to the beach for a couple of hours, or go for a bike ride, or to the cinema. I can do all that sort of stuff. On good days.'

'Only for a couple of hours?'

'Longer if there's a toilet at the beach, obviously. If there's a toilet I can spend all day there. Assuming there's toilet paper. And there's not a big queue. Always a good idea to carry toilet paper in your bag, actually. There's a top tip! When you think about it, that's a whole lot less to have to carry around than the spares *you* need with your ostomy. So, yeah, there's one of the instances where it's better.' She laughs, like it's cheered her right up.

I take her hint. I'm going to have to make up an emergency repair kit for school. 'What else?' I say grimly. 'What can't you eat and drink?'

'Some things are better, some worse. You don't have to chew food quite so obsessively as you do with a stoma – there aren't the same blockage issues. But you know when they tell you not to eat curry with your stoma because it might get under your flange and hurt your skin? Well, if you like curry, I suggest you have loads now. Because, trust me, the butt burn us pouch people get from not having a colon . . .' She sarcastically makes quote signs with her fingers and continues with her faultless impression of her mum's voice. '*To neutralise the caustic alkaline of everything coming straight out of your small intestine?* So, sooooo much worse when you add chilli fire!'

I've given up trying to make positive noises. This is just pure trauma. For both of us.

'My guts are killing me now so let's wrap this up,' she says dismissively.

'Wait. Can we talk about this after? You've dumped all this on me and . . . I was kind of hoping you'd tell me that I could get my bag reversed soon.'

'Sure! When I come back from warming the toilet seat for the tenth time today. I'll tell you that I *definitely* think you should get your ileostomy reversed as soon as you can. Don't wait the six months, jump the gun like me and get it next month even. Don't worry about getting everything healed and calmed down. Fuck it, you might even be lucky like me and get a fistula. You'll *love* the seton tube! And you said you played hockey? Great idea. Get rid of your bag and then you can kiss that goodbye. Make sure you listen to your stoma nurse and your surgeon and your mum. Because they know your body so much better than you do. They know that getting rid of your ostomy solves everything. They're the EXPERTS.' A spot of saliva pricks my face as she spits out the word 'experts'.

CHAPTER 23

We do actually have a chat when she comes back. And I don't know if it's because the gut cramping was making her particularly crazy before, but she ends up being nicer and does give me a couple of instances when she's been glad she didn't have her stoma anymore. She even reiterates that it's just her bad experience and her mum can vouch that plenty of people make the pouch work.

But then, after that glimmer of positivity, she finishes with the shit icing on the cake. If things don't get better, she might opt to have a permanent ileostomy like Chris.

And at least with an ostomy she can go to Glastonbury with her friends. Or she can stay over and share a bathroom with her best mate. Or even have sex! Because right now, she's not prepared to do any of that, for her own dignity.

I daren't breathe by this stage.

'Yeah,' she mutters. 'That's why I was so offended when

you rocked up acting the victim, wanting everyone to call you Shit Bag. Because I might get one again too.'

'Mel told me you had a chat,' Chris says later, when we're the first ones to sit down to afternoon tea in the canteen.

I nod and bite my bottom lip. I'm still shell-shocked after our conversation.

'I couldn't tell you,' he says, not letting my eyes go.

I pull a lopsided face and quietly admit, 'I probably wouldn't have listened anyway.'

'It doesn't have to mean the same for your situation. You know that?'

I don't answer, and prod the white spongy bread of my egg mayonnaise sandwich. It means *something* though. The surgeon and stoma nurse never told me any of those things. I've been blindly expecting to go back to normal when I get rid of my bag. I've been banking on it. So that I can get back to the way everything was before. *Who I was before*. I can't throw my whole life away and be someone new. I clutch my phone in my pocket and think of my friends, out there in Portugal.

'Where's Mel?' Chris says.

'What?' I quirk my lips. 'Oh, in the loo again probably.'

Chris shakes his head. 'We're nothing if not predictable.'

'Freya!' Jessica dumps an armful of coloured pens and

pencils and ostomy bags on the table. 'You didn't decorate Henry's bag yesterday!'

I catch Chris's eye as I say, 'Eh, yeah. Something came up.' I crank round, and sure enough wee Henners is standing just behind Jessica.

'You weren't at tea either,' she says shortly. 'Are you ill?'

'Not ill. But now's not a great time . . .'

Jessica hitches her butt up onto the edge of my chair. *Make yourself at home, why don't you? Please, leave me with my misery, Jessica!*

'Shall we maybe get you your own chair, Jessica?' Chris suggests. 'And one for Henry?' He sets them up either side of me, and moves to the opposite side of the table. Least he's not abandoning me to the whims of Jessica. But I wish he hadn't done that. 'Cause I'm trapped.

'Anyone hungry?' Chris hints, biting a sandwich.

'We're ready to decorate,' Jessica says decisively.

'Alright,' I say. This girl's a hard taskmaster! 'So, Henners? What're you thinking for your bag?'

The little boy's face lights up with excitement and he shifts his feet up onto the chair seat so he can reach the tabletop easier. 'Can I have a dinosaur?'

'Sure,' I say. 'What kind?'

'A tyrannosaurus!' He growls and bares his teeth.

Jessica squeals excitedly.

I laugh and pick up a black marker pen.

Chris says, 'Wow! You're getting a T-rex on your ostomy bag, Henry? I want a T-rex on my bag!'

Henners's eyes are the size of saucers.

Jessica says, all knowing, 'Chris has a permanent ostomy bag too, Henry, just like yours. Haven't you, Chris!'

I glance at Chris, raised eyebrows in solidarity. He's grinning at least. He breaks eye contact with me and says, 'That's correct, Jessica. My ileostomy is permanent.'

Our bag-decorating station has evolved now, so that me, Chris, Henners and Jessica each have a bag to decorate. And after a while I'm relieved I didn't go back to my cell to doom-scroll photos of everyone in Portugal. As promised, I'm decorating Henry's. Jessica is decorating mine. Chris is decorating one for Jessica, and Henry's decorating one for Chris. We have taped each bag with cream masking tape and we're only using the marker pens because we're worried that pencils might puncture the bags.

'So, Henry?' Chris says, all relaxed and chatty. 'What do you like to do in your free time when you're not an international spy?'

Henners does his signature squirm into his shell. But then he leans over to whisper to me so I can report back.

'Henry says he's not a spy – but that's what all spies say, isn't it, Chris – and he likes to play Roblox.' Henry whispers again. 'Henry was wondering what you like to do, Chris, when you're not an *internatural* spy?' Chris and I both have to hold our composure so we don't giggle at 'internatural'.

'I like to exercise in my free time, Henry. It makes my head clearer.'

Jessica scrunches her nose and says, 'I can't exercise. I'm not strong enough. I like to read instead. And watch superhero films. And I like cartoons.'

Chris and I lock eyes again, but this time we're not laughing. I don't know what Jessica's status is. But the fortified drink her mum brought over and the fact that she looks five but I've just found out she's almost eight hints that things aren't great for her.

'Did you know that Chris is going to play rugby with his ostomy bag?' I say. I don't mean it to make her feel bad, I just want her to feel hope.

'You can't play rugby with an ostomy,' Jessica says, like I'm an eejit.

'You can!' I say. 'Can't you, Chris!'

'I'm going to try,' he says.

'But you can't play proper rugby, like they do on the TV,' Jessica says, colouring in my bag. Her design so far looks like a red tablecloth floating above a pair of scissors, maybe . . . ?

'You'd be surprised what you can do with Crohn's or colitis, or an ostomy,' Chris says. 'And if you're not into sport, Jessica, well, you could be prime minister with one instead.'

Henners is back with the crockery-sized eyes. Only this time they're closer to side plates and I think I'm at dinner-plate dilation stage.

Jessica says what I'm thinking, 'You can't be prime minister with an ostomy!'

'Course you can!' Chris shifts his weight and fishes his phone out of his pocket. 'Let's have a look at who famous has had Crohn's or colitis, *or* an ostomy!'

Henners and Jessica are round Chris's side of the table in a shot to look at his phone.

Not wanting to be left out I open mine too.

And so we learn that Crohn's and colitis and ostomies aren't a new thing. And that we're in weighty company. Not only are many famous athletes and Olympians from all around the world afflicted with IBD or have ostomies, we discover YouTubers, actors, singers, comedians, magicians, biologists (Charles Darwin!), dancers (Fred Astaire) and – just like Chris said – world leaders! Multiple world leaders! Must be all the stress linked to running a country maybe? Dwight Eisenhower – US President – had a bag; also John F. Kennedy – US President – had colitis but not a bag; George Bush's son Marvin (not a president but his dad and brother were) had a bag; Napoleon Bonaparte! You know the weird hand in his waistcoat thing – rumour has it that that was to hide his goat-bladder ostomy bag! *WTF!* Mind blown. Queen Elizabeth II's mum reportedly had a bag. Prince Albert, Queen Victoria's husband, had Crohn's. Alfred the Great had Crohn's. And Shinzo Abe, the longest-serving Prime Minister of Japan who sadly was assassinated, had ulcerative colitis, like me!

I'm now feeling in strangely lofty company. Perhaps Jessica's superhero bags aren't so far off. Maybe I'm not disgusting having a bag I shit into. Maybe I'm just elite. And destined to take over the world!

CHAPTER 24

I'm gutted. It's over too quickly. One minute I'm in the common room offending Mel by insisting I'm called Shit Bag and the next I'm sitting round a blazing campfire on the last night with kids I can happily call my friends. Mel included.

My back hurts, my arms hurt, my legs hurt, even my feet hurt. But, amazingly, after adding canoeing and hiking in the rain (midgy fun that was) to the week and joining Chris for a jog (mostly walking) two of the mornings, my long scar doesn't hurt like it did and my legs aren't quite so brittle. I feel stronger. Chris can call me The Mighty Shit Bag after all.

We've all promised to stay in touch. But I wonder whether it's just good intentions. Will we see each other for real again after tomorrow lunchtime? Maybe if Chris gets back in the Merchants Firsts I really can watch him play rugby against Lowettsons.

'Do you want a wee snifter?' Mel says, nudging my elbow.

'What is it?'

'Vodka and Diet Coke.'

'I'm alright. Where did you get that?'

'Chris, come on, have a drink!' Mel shouts just a little too loud, considering her mum and dad are dancing on the opposite side of the campfire with a few of the parents and the younger kids. 'Come toast our ping-pong domination!' They – mostly Chris – won the final last night.

'You know my body's a temple, Mel,' Chris says.

'More like your body's boring,' Mel mutters. 'Come on, let's go dance,' she says, pulling Cody up. 'Coming?' she asks, flicking her hand at Chris.

'Not yet,' he says. 'My stoma's still a bit . . .'

She grimaces and rolls her eyes. 'You coming, Shit Bag? Show me your moves!'

'She needs to keep me company,' Chris says easily. 'Otherwise I'll be lonely.'

'We wouldn't want that, would we,' I say.

'Two boring bodies!' Mel wails.

'Owen! Come. Dance!' Mel demands. I watch all three of them go.

Now I know them better, Chris and Mel, I still feel they'd make a good couple. But Mel told me they'd always seen the other like a sibling. They're family.

173

We also had a chat about her pouch this afternoon. It's settled a little over the last two days, so she's being more positive. I'm holding on to that glimmer of hope. To get me through heading home, back to my old life.

'She's wrecked,' Chris says, leaning back to lay his arm along the felled tree trunk we've all been using as a support. But he sits up again and touches his side.

'You hurting?' I ask.

'Hmh. Still kicking myself for that stupid handstand dive.'

'You don't think you should talk to the stoma nurse about it?'

'I'm alright for now.'

'Okay . . . If only you'd followed me and Mel's stylish leads into the water,' I say, shaking my head earnestly.

Chris sticks his tongue out at me.

'Will that stop you playing rugby?' I ask.

'Don't know. Might just be a pulled muscle. I probably need to start being more positive.'

This surprises me. 'You don't think you're positive?'

He smiles. 'Not as much as I was a year ago, Shit Bag. Do you think I'm positive?'

I draw a pattern in the sand. 'Yeah, I do. Least you're *trying* to play rugby. I've surrendered to the fact that my ex-best-friend – the one who's with my ex-boyfriend – well,

I haven't told you, but it turns out she's taken my hockey position so yeah . . . guess that's that.'

Chris looks at me for a beat longer than feels low-key. 'That's shit,' he finally says.

'Yeah, it is a bit.' I throw the stick I've been drawing with at the fire, but it just lands midway on the sand.

Chris rests back against the wood and then suddenly leans against me.

'Hey!' I say.

'What?' he says teasingly.

'Nothing . . .' I say it while thinking how much I like it when he touches me. Even if it is to squash me.

'You know,' he says, shifting to lean on his elbow and fiddle with the end of my hoodie's drawstring between his fingertips. 'You *could* play hockey this term. If you've not completely conceded defeat to the exes?'

'Course I could!' I say sarcastically, keeping absolutely still so he doesn't drop the drawstring joining us.

But Chris's face doesn't break into that easy wide grin that I'm used to. And I realise he's waiting for my reaction.

'Urr, giant abdominal scar, remember? Brand-new ostomy. Physically resembling a teenage Groot?'

He laughs at that. 'A cute Groot.'

'You think I'm cute?'

'In an angry Groot-having-a-temper-tantrum kind of way, yep.'

I inhale sharply, pretending to be offended. Then say, 'Why, thank you. That's the nicest thing anyone's ever said to me!'

He chuckles. 'Seriously though, you could do it. Your surgeon must think your scar's sound enough – they let you go canyoning. And, no offence, but hockey isn't rugby!'

I gnaw on my lip and start biting the skin around my nails. And stop to say, 'I'm not fit enough. They've been training in Portugal all week.'

'You've been *here* all week. Don't you feel stronger and fitter after all the activities we've been doing?'

'Yeah. I do . . .'

'And why do you think I got you jogging the last two mornings?'

'Because you enjoyed my company?'

'God, no!'

'Rude!' I laugh.

Chris tugs on the end of the drawstring, so I have to look at him properly. 'Joking aside,' he says quietly, 'if you're anything like me then it must be killing you that you can't play your favourite sport. They're not just teammates, are they? I don't know who I am anymore without them. They're my life. Like family. The whole thing is life.'

That's vast! Eyes locked on Chris's, I'm remembering

how he seemed to know what I couldn't say about my fears and happiness the other day. It turns out I really didn't have to voice that I'm lost. That I don't know where I fit. Because he feels the same. And all over again, I'm blinking furiously.

'Sorry. I didn't mean to . . .' His arm is suddenly around me and he squeezes me briefly to his side.

'It's okay,' I say, barely moving. Intensely aware of my every breath, of his arm guarding my back. 'I agree. I'm just . . .' I pull my sleeve over my hand and wipe my eyes. 'Feeling sorry for myself, probably.'

He says quietly, 'We all feel sorry for ourselves at one stage or another.'

We sit in bolstered silence for a little while looking at the fire. I don't think we need to explain anything more to each other.

'So I wasn't *really* planning on making you cry tonight,' he says.

'No? What *was* your plan?'

'Well . . .' He lifts the metal end of the drawstring again with his left hand and twists it between his thumb and forefinger. But really I'm thinking about his other hand, still holding me. 'First, I was going to get you all riled up to want to play hockey.'

I am suitably riled. Just not because of hockey. I feel like I'm melting. Losing all my rigid form.

'And then . . .' he tails off.

'Then?' I say impatiently.

'Then I was going to ask you for your socials @s so we could maybe meet up when we're back at school.'

Electric static shorts my chest, over my scalp, down my arms.

He says, 'But Mel already shared all our contacts so, yeah . . .'

So? What do you mean – yeah? Are we still meeting? He's not moving. I realise he's waiting for me to react. He's teasing me. My fizzing nerves turn to a steely calm. And, I sly side-eye him, as I say deadpan, 'Well, that's a bit different to what I had planned.'

'Yeah?' he murmurs. 'What did *you* have planned?'

'I did actually plan on making you cry!'

He pulls away from me. 'Shit Bag! You're savage!' But then he pushes my arm good-naturedly. I nudge him back. We have this odd but kind of thrilling push and pull of bumping each other with our elbows and shoulders.

Until we stop.

I feel breathless and all my nerves are alive. I scan beyond the campfire, where everyone's laughing and dancing. No one's looking at us.

Wanting to touch him again, I say, 'Yup. That's me, savage by name, savage by nature!' Adding recklessly, 'But you love it, don't you!'

He doesn't say anything at first. The wrestling energy has gone. Dissipated like the woodsmoke from the fire. I have to look though. And in this light he's all aquamarine eyes and rose-gold Scottish gloaming on his skin.

Then he stretches out his hand and touches my face with his fingertips, and I want to shiver all over but I don't move – no, I *move*, everything moves – inside – but on the outside I hide it, because he's stroking my earlobe . . . and he says, 'Do you want to go for a walk?'

I nod, not trusting my voice.

We walk, barely apart, down to the beach. Our den's just ahead. 'Do you want to go inside?' Chris asks.

'Let's go paddle in the loch first.'

I yank off my trainers, shove my phone and hoodie on top of them, and wade into the water without hesitation. It's cold. Like a shot of being alive has just been injected between my toes and it's rushing up to my heart.

Chris steps in more gingerly. Grinning at me but looking down on every step deeper like he's afraid there's a poisonous spiny creature lurking ready to spike him.

Water up to my knees now – it's testament to my increasing confidence that I've been wearing shorts for the last three days – I shiver. But the prickling nerves and hairs on end just make me feel even more excited about being here. With Chris. Feeling this tension between us. Drawing closer.

Since that first day in the common room when he laughed at me calling myself Shit Bag. Allowing me comfort in being myself. Even if I don't know who that is. Not yet! Maybe that's what this is. A new beginning. Am I being reborn . . . ?

And with that thought, I do something mad. I drop back into the frigid water and kick out, swimming on my back.

I realise too late, like someone who's jumped in the pool and forgotten their phone in their pocket, that the edge of my flange and the fabric backing of my bag are going to be soaking and itchy all night now. But fuck it. What's done is done. I move more upright in the water so that I can look for Chris and I'm surprised to see him swimming towards me.

He gasps. 'You're mad! This – is – free-zing!'

I grin. 'Our bags! Are. Go-ing. To be. Wet.'

'You think—!'

We're both kicking, grinning and treading loch water.

'Now what?' Chris says.

I'm frozen. And I'm tired. This is a workout in itself. But I gasp, suddenly knowing what I want to do next.

'What—?'

'Come on!' I swim back to the water's edge and manage to get out stiffly. Chris links arms with me and we both laugh as we slither and slide over the mossy, weedy stones, until we're back on the sand. He looks at me expectantly.

I put my finger to my lips then gather up my hoodie, phone and shoes and walk with stiff, cold legs to our den. But I don't go inside.

'Aren't you freezing?' Chris says. I hold out my hand. He closes his fingers around it. 'You're frozen! We need to go back to the lodge.'

'You remember that "fears and happiness" exercise the other day?' I say.

'Eh? Yeah?'

I don't answer and instead beckon for him to follow me. And I take off across the sand, breaking cover, heading for the wooden cabins.

Water running hot, I wave my arms towards the outdoor shower, as if I'm a magician's assistant.

Chris blinks and bites his bottom lip.

'I thought we could warm up,' I explain.

He nods. And his eyebrows do something tense, wrinkling his forehead.

'Is this okay?' I ask.

He grins. 'It's very okay, Shit Bag!'

'Good,' I say simply. 'I'm going to go empty my bag. Be back in a sec.' I go into the loos, empty my bag and I'm back out within a minute. Chris must've gone to do the same because the shower's empty but still running. Really feeling the cold now, I step into the water. I can remove my T-shirt and shorts after this, and pull on my hoodie so I don't get hypothermia on the walk back to the lodge.

'Hey!' Chris says, making me jump.

'Fancy seeing you here!' I say, hoping he'll remember that those were his exact words the day he set up the shower for me. The day he rescued me.

He steps in closer so that the warm water hits the front of his T-shirt. Water droplets bead on the end of his dark eyelashes. He shivers and clenches his fingers as if he's praying. 'Oh, that feels good . . .'

I quirk a smile and close my eyes to the water running over my face, marvelling at this moment in time that I somehow have got myself in. And I reach out and touch the waistband of his shorts for balance.

As if I've said it's okay in that touch, I feel Chris's fingers slide around my lower back, wet skin on exposed wet skin briefly making contact. And we move closer. To hug. Standing together under the warm water.

'So,' I finally say, looking up, tipping my head back, so that I can feel the stretch at my throat, to see his eyes. Deep aquamarine, like I could swim in them. Surely they'd be warmer than the loch?

'So?' he says, a quirk teasing the side of those lips. Fuller than other lips I've encountered. Always amused. Maybe it's the dimples at the sides that do it.

I answer. 'I've worked out what I want to achieve before I leave here.'

'What's that then?' his voice croaks.

'I want to kiss you.'

Chris frowns. 'Weird . . .'

My breath catches – *I've got this wrong.*

But then he says, 'I've been thinking about my original answer. And seeing that I've managed to injure myself doing handstands already, I was working towards a similar objective.'

'Were you now?'

'Yes. I was.'

'Hmm . . .'

His lips are fighting that grin of his, they crack lopsided.

I'm fighting a grin myself. 'You sure you're not just copying me?' I manage, partly straight-faced.

'Hmm? Maybe you're copying me. When exactly did you decide you wanted to kiss me?' he says, all serious.

'Umm . . . ?'

He laughs. 'Don't answer that, Shit Bag. I have little doubt I win that one.'

'Why?' I'm genuinely confused.

'Because I wanted to kiss you the first time you sat down beside me and announced you're Shit Bag!'

'*That's* what made you want to kiss me?' I say, incredulous.

A flash of white teeth with his smile. 'That and the way you are.'

I process this for a moment, just staring up into his eyes. 'What way am I?'

He pulls me closer for a moment, a brief squeeze of warmth. 'Let me see,' he says. 'You're quite . . . *unique*.'

'Unique?'

'You're a force of nature.'

'Like a natural disaster? Hurricane Freya?'

He tips his head back, laughing, and chokes when he gets a mouthful of water. 'Exactly,' he says, clearing his voice. 'You swept in, raged for a while and swept out, leaving devastation in your wake.'

'That doesn't sound especially desirable.'

His grin settles into a softer expression. 'You're *desirable*! In lots of ways. Your eyes for one are striking. They're like ice. Or . . . a White Walker's!'

'A White Walker—?'

He laughs. 'A sexy White Walker.'

I grumble, 'Guess I'm still bony like a White Walker too.'

He ducks down a little so we're at similar eye levels. 'Freya, look at me.'

'What?'

'You and me. We're the same. You know?'

'Obviously. We have poo bags.'

184

'Yeah. We do,' he says seriously. 'But I don't mean that. I mean . . . everyone else is judging us. Because we're different.'

I blink a few times, biting at my bottom lip. How does he always seem to know what I'm thinking?

'Let's not do that anymore,' he says. 'Not to ourselves and not to each other. We are who we are.' He stays there, hunkered down waiting for me to nod. When I reluctantly give in, he says, 'Good.'

'Anyway,' he says, 'it's the other things that make me want to spend time with you.'

'Like what? My dragon breath? My greyscale skin?'

'All of those. Yeah,' he nods seriously. 'It's definitely your greyscale skin that makes me want to kiss you. I can't wait for that to spread across my own face. You're infectious.' He smiles. 'It's more that you're real!'

I feel the warmth from his eyes spread through me.

'You're flawed. You're passionate. Outspoken. Honest. Funny. And, most especially, you're a little shitbag at times. But that's what makes you authentic. That's what makes me want to kiss you right now.'

And he leans down and closes his lips over mine and steals my breath away.

CHAPTER 25

'Morning, Shit Bag!' Chris sing-songs, knotting the cord at the waistband of his trackie bottoms as I skip down the slope to the kids' play area. 'I was starting to think you'd gone back to sleep.'

'I thought about it,' I say lightly. I didn't sleep though. Not a bit. I just lay awake, my stomach and nerves going crazy, unable to believe what happened last night. Even now, my head and limbs are ringing fresh with it. The only reason I'm late is my stoma moved just before I was about to head down, and then once I'd been to empty my bag I got caught up in front of the mirror wondering how to make my hair look less like a seven-year-old page boy at a family wedding, and whether I had time to go get my mascara to make my White Walker eyes pop. I didn't.

'Aren't you sore?' I say, sitting down on the rubber safety surface around the swings to tie my laces properly.

'Affirmative. Why did you let me do those backflips last night?'

'Hey! Don't blame me for you immediately abandoning your resolution to *not* do a backflip as soon as Mel egged you on with her crap cartwheels. That was entirely your fault.'

'It was all to impress you though, Shit Bag. Every bit of my stupidity. Are you telling me it worked, and you adore me?' he teases.

His words creep down my back and wrap round me. At this time in the morning, it's an unexpected sensation. Attraction. Proper, deep attraction. I didn't expect this to happen here. I'm not entirely sure *what* has happened while I've been here. But I know I feel different about myself and my life in general too.

I feel upbeat.

The opposite of how I felt when I arrived.

Only I don't know how easy it will be for me to carry this home. Into the real world. To my old life. To my family and friends. Where do Chris and me fit into all that?

But right now, before everyone else wakes, perhaps this is what we need – to connect – before we brave the real world . . .

'For sure, you're adorable,' I say, trying to pull my jumbled thoughts together. 'And your pain this morning is very *impressive*.'

'It is a bit,' Chris says. He hitches his T-shirt and, gritting his teeth, yanks off his black support belt. 'This doesn't feel like a pulled muscle anymore.' He prods around, along his abs. The area down the side of his bag looks raised compared with the rest of his stomach. But it might be a trick of the morning sunshine.

Unpeeling my eyes from his stomach, I say, 'Should we cancel our run?'

'Hell, no! You're not getting out of it that easily, Shit Bag. You've got a hockey team to get fit for . . .' He grimaces, pulling an ugly-pretty snarl of discomfort. Only it's not remotely ugly. It just makes me want to focus on his lips for a really long time.

'Well, as long as we're clear,' I say. 'Backflips are out. Just in case you were going to suggest I add those to my training regime!'

'Woaw? So you're in? You're going to play hockey?'

'I *might*. But no backflips!'

'Don't worry. I don't think I'll be doing a backflip myself ever again,' he says. 'I solemnly promise we'll keep upright for today's training.'

I get another glimpse of his scar-free, perfect tummy. When I say perfect tummy, that's with the exception of that little thing called an ileostomy bag that happens to be blocking about a quarter of his ripped, dark-tan torso. And suddenly I'm thinking of exercising lying down.

He'd see my scar though.

'You don't have the scar I do!' I blurt, like I'm revealing a dark secret, even though he already knows about it. 'Do you want to see it?'

He's surprised – so am I. Why did I offer to show him my scar? But then he smiles and says, 'I saw it a little when you showed me your bag at the shower.' He looks flustered, and says earnestly, 'I'd very much like to have a proper look at your scar. If you're okay showing me?'

'Yeah . . .' And as soon as I say this, I get that creeping sensation over my body again. It's not a bad, creeped-out feeling. More, *I'm nervous and my stomach's turning-like-a-washing-machine-on-spin-cycle* feeling.

'You don't have to show me, Freya.'

'I know. I want to.' Still, I haven't lifted my top. I'm actually shy! I force my hand to take hold of the hem of my T-shirt and lift it.

I can't look at him.

I keep my eyes down, staring at the view that's been my private everything for the last two months. It's changed. No more is the skin iodine stained, the centre line two pieces of meat, held together only by a crooked train track of staples.

Staples.

A sight you see on school handouts. Never meant for a child's skin. Or a teenager's . . .

My stomach. No longer a part of my body I take for granted either. Just there before, with a belly button in the middle. Instead now, the belly button is pulled squint by this healing scar. And the scar. A livid purple line. Will it fade, will it turn pale like my skin? Will it always tug? Restrict my movement? Never let me forget?

Chris moves closer. I focus on the white Nike swoosh on the hip of his tracksuit. Wait for his assessment of me.

'It's nice and neat,' he says.

'You think?'

'Yeah, I've seen a few that burst open.'

'Have you? Where?'

'Online. I think it's common to get a bit of infection – you know, when you're run down after the surgery – and they lay it open to drain so the scar when it heals doesn't look so perfect.'

Perfect? 'So, it looks . . . okay?'

'Yeah, it looks really good!'

I pat my stomach, oddly proud. 'Yeah?' I look up at him. He beams back.

And again, I'm hit by how grateful I feel for my experiences here at camp. For the support Chris has given me throughout. The way he's made me feel safe. Respected. Desirable, even.

I reach up on tiptoe to kiss him, and say, 'Thanks!'

* * *

'Come on, Slowpoke!' I pant as we scramble up the hill behind the beach and car park. But when I turn, I see that Chris isn't with me. He's back down the grassy bank, hunched over. 'You alright?' I shout.

He doesn't reply until I slide down beside him. 'Not really,' he says, moving his hands slowly onto the ground and edging more upright.

'What is it?'

He groans, his face scrunched as if he's blinded by the glare of the sun, but the way he's cradling his stomach I realise it's from pain.

'Undo your belt.'

He paws at his T-shirt like it hurts so bad that his fingers are paralysed.

'Here. Lie back. Can you . . . ?' That even seems too much for him. 'I'll take it off, okay?' He lifts his eyebrows in silent agreement and the movement momentarily clears the tension from his face as if things aren't so bad. But as I take a hold of the overlapping tab on the Velcro belt to release the pressure, his knee recoils.

'Agh. Shit! Don't. Fu—'

'Okay, okay, I won't . . .'

He's rolling foetal on his side, but as he writhes he manages to yank the belt free. 'Nngh! Shiiit.' He groans, grinding his head back into the peaty earth.

'Is it your stoma or something else?' I rush, as if saying it fast makes it easier for him to hear.

'Don't know. Can you— Nngh! Someone.'

'Okay.' But it's not. 'I don't have my phone. Is yours here?' His contorted fingers poke his pocket. I get his phone out and fumble to try and unlock it, but I can see there's no reception anyway. 'No reception. Shall I run back? Maybe I can help you walk. I don't want to leave . . .' I pat his shoulder as if it's molten to the touch.

'I – can't walk . . .' he pants.

'Okay. Okay. I'm going. Here, I'll put your phone there. Just in case it starts working.'

He's in too much pain to respond. I press my lips to his cheek, and slip away down the bank towards the path and then, like it's vitally important that I say bye properly, I scuttle up again beside him and murmur in his ear, 'I won't be long.' And I kiss him on the lips, trying to be gentle but knowing I'm wasting time. I draw away but he grabs my arm, staring at me with cold, panicked eyes in a lifetime-microsecond. Then I leave him to toboggan back down the slope.

I haven't managed to run further than about fifty metres so far this week. Not without slowing to a walk for the same distance to recover, but I can't waste time now. Maybe his gut's ruptured like mine did and it's quickly poisoning his insides.

It feels like the air's sandpapering along my throat and into my lungs. The shingle's worse than the sand.

I'm stumbling like I'm drunk, legless.

My tears slip cold towards my ears.

I'm running in slow motion. On a treadmill going nowhere.

I have to stop at the little bridge over the stream, to cough and spit bloody, metallic phlegm. And wheeze air into my concrete lungs. We kissed here last night. When we walked back to the lodge shivering and giggling. I can't move yet. I need breath. Get my legs to harden from jelly. Find something beyond trembling.

And I stumble on, along the rough rocky edge of the loch. Slipping over slimy moss and algae. Sobbing and whimpering.

'Some – bo-dy—' I pant as I get into reception. It's empty. I lean over, my hands on my knees. 'Ngh!' I cough to clear the clog of phlegm from my throat. 'Somebody help!' I manage a little louder. I exhale as much as I can, like the physio taught me to cough up crap from my lungs after my surgery, and with one massive inhale of breath, I shout, 'SOMEBODY HELP ME!' And with one more inhale I let out the best scream I can offer, 'AAAAAHH!'

* * *

The adults take over. Running and grabbing and controlling their voices. Rewording my incoherent directions in the ambulance call. Driving the tree-shaded driveway, swinging round bends, onto a rough farm road banked by moss-covered dykes, rickety wire fencing . . .

And all I can think of is Chris writhing on his side, and the machine Annabelle put in the boot, never seen in real life but familiar from every fictional A&E resuscitation.

It can't be that bad.

He wasn't having a heart attack. It's his tummy. Like me. I didn't die. I'm here. He must still be here too.

And there he is. Still writhing in pain.

But the others know what to do. And I pace behind, looking between, to catch a glimpse. To connect. Before he's ripped away.

And then the ambulance is here. I was wrong when I saw the access road, that first day we came to the beach. The ambulance doesn't need to drive down the road to get here, because the ambulance is a helicopter.

The crew give Chris an injection of the good stuff, block his face with an oxygen mask and, before I can think straight, he's away in a bluster of wind and slashing blades.

* * *

Cody and Mel meet me on the path, and Mel clamps her arms around my neck like a vice and demands, 'Tell me he's okay.'

'I don't know,' I falter.

'We'll know more once he gets to Glasgow,' Annabelle says behind me.

'Do you think we'll ever see him again?' Cody says.

I drop my hands and look at her. I don't know what to say to that. I just know that I feel sick, shaky and numb. And afraid. Afraid that when I wondered yesterday whether I'd ever see Chris again perhaps it was a premonition. A premonition that I won't.

We're subdued when we say our goodbyes: Mel, me, Cody, Owen, little Jessica and Henners. Henners solemnly offers me his gift. A decorated ostomy bag. He's drawn a picture of me and some sort of animal on all fours, beside a pointy tepee? 'What's that, Henners? Is it a dog?'

'No!' he says, as if I'm the dumbest person he's ever met. 'That's Chris. You're doing your exercises. This is the swings. And the sun. And grass. And that's a bottle of that pink stuff he drinks.'

'Thanks, Henners,' I say, hugging the little kid tight. When I release him, I'm blind with tears.

'As soon as anyone hears from Chris, we message

195

everyone,' Mel instructs. I'm so thankful Mel set up our chat group last night. Already there are a ton of messages waiting for Chris.

We all nod, and soon it's just her and me, clearing the last of our stuff from our cell. I puff my breath out. 'Give me a hug, will you?'

Mel complies. 'He'll be okay,' she says.

'He'd better be!'

'Soon as Mum knows more, I'll message you first.'

'Thanks.'

'He was really happy about what happened last night.'

'He told you?'

She nods. 'Don't fuck him around, Shit Bag. He's one of the good ones. The best!'

CHAPTER 26

Mum waits until we're almost home and on the Edinburgh bypass before she tells me, 'We're going to the Millings' later this afternoon for a barbecue.'

I shake my head that I'm not going, and look out the window again at the blur of cars.

'You threw a tantrum, Freya, because we *didn't* go to the last one. Ems organised this especially for you. You're coming.'

And here it is. Everything I wanted. Craved. I'm going to see Lockie today.

But that was before Chris. Still no news from him.

They expect me to return to my old life, the day to day, family, friends, exes, like none of this week has happened? It doesn't work like that. You can't show me the way forward and then expect me to turn back and walk into the past.

And I was okay to be Shit Bag at camp. I asked for it. Actively encouraged it. I was among allies. Safe. And they all understood, or at least tried to understand. We were equals. In one way or another.

But that's not gonna be the case in the real world. Back home. At school. They don't understand. They don't care. *They're* calling me Shit Bag!

And where's that coming from? The privileged position of never having had an ostomy!

Who do they think they are to do that?

That's a name reserved for use by a different type of privileged few. Yeah, maybe I am Shit Bag. But only to the elite.

My head's a mess. Can't think straight. I don't know what I want. It's a jumble of emotions.

Come on, Chris! Just message you're okay. Maybe my brain will stop hurting if I know you're okay.

Mel's message comes in as we're driving to Lockie's house.

> **Mel:** He's in surgery! Mum says we won't hear anything more for a few hours. Suspected twisted gut and a hernia. Will let you know any updates. Mx

Surgery? My twisted gut untwisted naturally. If Chris is having surgery, his must be much worse. Or is it for his hernia? How am I supposed to go make small talk? See Lockie. When Chris is unconscious on an operating table!

But next thing I know, we're parking beside the kitchen window at the Millings' house. Mum's refusing to take me home. And just being here . . . my head's bombarding me with memories.

I scan the cars looking for Morven's parents'. But I don't see theirs.

'Is anyone else from school invited?' I say to Mum.

'Briony said they're going to her parents for a week before you're back to school, so Morven isn't here. I don't know about the MacKays. Can't see their car . . .'

Meathead better not be coming. I can't handle seeing him, the way I'm feeling today. I'll end up stabbing him in the eye with a lamb kebab skewer.

Suriya?

Mum and Dad get out of the car. I remain in the back seat. It's only just crossed my mind that Suriya could be here. And then I feel it. The hot flooding sensation on my stomach. My stoma has moved. Loads. I look down at the waist of my baggy cargo pants and there's a bulge where my bag is. Fuck. Why now?

Mum opens my door. 'Are you getting out or shall I tell Ems you'll eat in here?'

'Oh, Freya, love, you're looking much more yourself,' Ems, Lockie's mum, croons, holding me at arm's length. I tug at the bottom of my vest top. 'And look at that tiny waist.' She hugs me again, still barely making any body contact for fear of breaking me. Ems moves onto Mum. 'You look rested,' she says, hugging Mum tight.

'It's just what we needed. All of us,' Mum adds, with what could almost be mistaken for a smile in my direction.

I make wide eyes at her and she finally remembers what she's supposed to be asking.

'Ems,' Mum says. 'Can Freya use your en suite?'

'Oh, of course, love! Here, come with me.' I follow Ems up the stairs to their bedroom. I know the way. I know where everything is in this house. But I let her show me where her en suite is, let her check there's plenty of loo roll etc. for me, because I don't want to meet Lockie on my own. I'd rather have Ems as a buffer. A human shield.

'Ems?' I say when she heads out into her room. 'Is anyone else coming from school today?'

'No, love. It's just you and Lockie.' She smiles sadly. 'Maybe you can have a nice talk together.'

I nod, say, 'Thanks,' and close the door. I take a deep,

staggered breath and close my eyes. I'm glad there won't be anyone else here from school. But Lockie's here. He's enough to have my heart pounding and my guts twisting. And twisting guts has me thinking of Chris again. This is one almighty head-fuck. No updates.

Once I'm done, washed my hands, sprayed lots of the bathroom air freshener and opened the window to let the room breathe, I realise that I can look out onto the garden from this window. I scan the different groups, searching for Lockie. There are younger kids messing around on the rope swing over by the big conker tree. And then I see him from behind. He's wearing a white linen shirt. His neck is tanned. Hair looks blonder. He's making up a drink. Turns. Two drinks in hands. Fringe and freckled nose are briefly visible before he walks towards the house and out of my view.

Heart racing, I lean on the vanity unit. Regard myself in the mirror. How does he still have this effect on me? After everything he's done. After everything we seem to do to each other. The disaster couple. But every time we come back for more.

Well, we used to.

Totally toxic.

I focus properly on my appearance. I'm so pale compared with his tan. Sickly and fine-boned. Delicate. This wispy fringe! I hate it! I have a few more freckles from being outside. Should've brought more make-up for touch-ups. I open drawers. Find a pot of cream bronzer. Put a blob on my shaking index finger and create a bronzed edge to my already smudged smoky eye. Sea salt hairspray. Scrunch some into my hair for texture. Tester perfume down the front of my lace-edged vest top and around my belly and ostomy – just to be sure I don't stink. Stand side-on. Least I'm looking flat-stomached now I've emptied my bag.

Out on the landing, I listen. Can hear Ems talking downstairs.

And then there's white shirt and blond hair, rolled sleeves, tanned forearms bounding up the stairs, and on the turn he stops dead, grabs the banister and stares at me.

'Hello . . .' I say.

'Hi . . .' he says, taking a step up. His tan is well roasted.

I regret wearing baggy trousers. I feel frumpy. I fold my arms and say, all energy-drink bright, 'How was Portugal?'

'Mint! How was . . . ?' He hasn't a clue where I've been.

'Good, thanks.' I clear my throat. 'Is Suriya here?' There you go. I've said her name now. What've you got to say for yourself?

Lockie's sunburn deepens. 'No. She's not here.'

'Oh, why not?' I say.

'She wasn't invited.' He folds his arms and leans his hip against the banister.

'Trouble in paradise?' This is not what I planned. It really isn't. I was going to be completely chill with them as a couple. We were already split. And he ghosted me and called me Shit Bag! What do I care who he pulls? I have Chris . . .

I quickly fish out my phone and check for an update. Nothing. I put it away.

'You want some privacy?' Lockie says.

'No. Had more than enough *privacy* from you lately, thanks.' I can't stop myself. My bitterness cup runneth over.

'Maybe we need to talk.'

'Maybe we do.'

'Let's go in my room then.'

'Lead the way.'

'Okay. I'll just . . .' He edges round me. Not touching. Still repulsed by me then? Still repulsed by my shit bag?

I do my usual and lie on his bed. It's not in the slightest bit appropriate but for some reason I'm feeling light-headed.

'Make yourself at home.'

'I already have.'

'Actually, I need a drink for this. Do you want a Diet Coke?'

'Yeah – no. You got any cordial? Flat cordial?'

'Elderflower?'

'Yeah. That'll do.'

'Okay.' He sighs to himself before he leaves his room.

I fold my arms and wait for a bit. Then I turn my face, bury it in his pillow and inhale. A thousand memories. Brought on by Lockie's smell, so familiar. Just him. I grasp the pillow and grind it into my face. It hurts. Here. Twisted in his duvet. I remember the months of campaigning he put in to get this double bed. The plans we made of what would happen here. What did happen.

I roll off the bed and stand. Make things look straight, normal. No point in thinking about what's been and gone. But then the weirdest thing happens – my whole body shivers. Not from cold but from a welling-up of something physical. Like my body's not buying my denial. Being here, again, after everything I've been through, is a massive fucking deal! It maybe looks the same in here. But nothing's the same. I'm changed. Evolved. And at least my body knows it. Even if my head's gaslighting me.

I check my phone again. Still nothing. I message Mel:

> **Me:** Hey. You've not heard anything more, have you?

Mel: Not yet. Mum says his mum'll have more important things to worry about than updating us.

Me: Could we call the hospital to check he's alive?

Mel: Of course he's alive, you nutter!

Me: Yeah, but we don't know that for sure.

Mel: You home?

Me: No. At my ex-boyfriend's house.

Mel: Why? Isn't he the one who called you Shit Bag? And pulled your friend!! What about Chris? Not chill, Shit Bag.

Me: Mum and Dad brought me to a family barbecue. Our parents are best friends. And I'm about to have a showdown with him over All Of The Above.

Mel: Okay . . . As I said, don't fuck Chris around.

Me: I'm not. Let me know as soon as you know. Please!

'Alright, Mum!' Lockie shouts out on the landing.

I close my phone and slide it into the thigh pocket of my cargos.

Lockie bumps in through the door and sets a tray down on his desk. 'Your mum says you have to eat.'

I swallow the lump in my throat. 'Right . . .'

'That's for you.' He hands me a plate with a mountain of food: couple of burgers, sausage, white bun, chicken thigh, pasta and lettuce leaves.

I perch on the side of his bed and try and cut a burger into quarters.

'Can I sit there too, or do you want me to sit at my desk?'

'Knock yourself out.' I'm so, so tempted to say – *No, literally! Why don't you knock yourself out?* Instead, I put a piece of burger in my mouth and chew.

Lockie stacks his own burgers and bun into a double cheeseburger with salad and guacamole and God knows what else and practically dislocates his jaw to take a bite. He nods to himself, bouncing the bed in the process, as he chews. Just like old times. *Jolly, jolly old times.* I shove another bit of burger into my mouth and chew more savagely.

'Your juice is there,' he says with a full mouth.

'Thanks.' I can't be bothered to retrieve it from the tray. Anyway, the way I'm feeling right now there's a high chance I'll just throw it at him. I stab the sausage and eat it the way you see in cartoons. 'Can I have a bit of your cucumber?'

He nods, because he's just taken another bite.

I steal two bits of cucumber and chew on them thoroughly before swallowing.

'Do you want some of my coleslaw?'

'I can't.'

He chews faster and swallows. 'I don't really understand what you can and can't have.' He's got a drip of ketchup on the side of his mouth.

'No. I don't imagine you do. You haven't been around me much lately. Been keeping yourself busy with a certain *other* friend.'

Lockie drops the remnants of his burger onto his plate with a sigh and sets it on the floor. 'Okay, come on. Let's do this. Tell me what a dick I've been and that you never want to speak to me ever again. Get it all out. Because whatever you say it's not going to be any worse than what I've already said to myself. I'm ashamed. There, I've said it. I'm the lowest of the low. Scum.'

If I were my mother, I'd be lifting just one eyebrow right now. I'm not sure what I'm achieving with my own face, but I stare at him for a bit and then blink.

'I was upset – she was upset – and it happened. But that's no excuse.'

'Oh, you were both upset . . .'

'For you. We were upset for you.'

'Right. So it's my fault that you pulled Suriya.' I stand quickly and clatter my plate onto the tray. 'Because you were both *upset* – for me – you had to console one another by meeting in secret and completely blanking me? And

208

what about Shit Bag?' It's like a sucker punch to my chest, saying my nickname in front of him, picturing that meme Meathead sent out. All the likes. The disgusting comments. Knowing he started it. 'I feel sick,' I mumble, and find my way back onto the edge of his bed.

'Do you want me to get your mum and dad?'

'No! You don't get out of this that easily. Pass me your bin.'

He does, but it's woven so I'm not sure it's going to be much good. I lean my head on it for a while. By the time I sit up, my eyes are foggy with tears. 'I can't believe you started that—' My voice breaks.

Lockie slides towards me. 'Frey—'

'Don't! Don't you touch me! You've lost that privilege.'

'Okay, but don't cry then. You know I can't handle it when you cry.'

'Don't cry? Don't – cry? If you can't handle me crying, Lockie, maybe you shouldn't've called me Shit Bag, let Meathead spread it round the entire school and totally ghosted me. Or started going out with Suriya!'

'We're not going out.'

That stumps me. I formulate a couple of insults but they don't come out of my mouth. Finally I manage, 'Just shagging?'

'What?' Lockie lurches to his feet. 'No. Is that what she said?'

'I don't know what she's said. We're not friends anymore, remember. Or had that not crossed your mind? Did you expect us to be a happy little harem of friends?'

'Well, no,' he blusters. 'And we only snogged . . . and stuff.'

And stuff . . . 'Guh, I'm going to be sick.' I retch and feel the burger-sausage-cucumber combo jump threateningly.

'I'm getting your parents.'

'Don't you fucking dare!' Strangely the rush of rage to my head makes me feel less queasy. I puff my cheeks.

'Do you want a drink?'

'Yeah.' I stick my hand out. He fetches the glass and edges it between my fingers. I take a sip. I'm feeling really quite queasy now. It's been a long and stressful day. Like I've crossed the divide between two parallel universes. The safety and security of camp with Chris, now turned into a nightmare, and here, in this intimate, familiar room, with Lockie, feeling wrong and foreign.

I lean on the bin and watch him as I drink the cordial. 'I still can't believe you called me Shit Bag. The one person in the world I thought I could trust.'

'It wasn't like that, Freya. I just . . .' He scrubs his hand through his hair and it flops for a moment out of place so it looks ridiculous. Then of course it flops back into place. 'I didn't mean it like that. I happened to make a throwaway comment that you can be a shitbag at times and it was taken out of context. And so you are, sometimes. You shout at me when I'm late. Or my phone dies. Or me and the lads want to go and watch sport. It wasn't because of . . .' Lockie gestures towards my tummy, the exact place where my bag is. Because he knows where it is, he visited me in the High Dependency ward. I grate my front teeth against my bottom lip. Liar.

'Meathead just latched onto the words, and I couldn't get him to stop.'

'Bullshit! If you wanted Meathead to stop calling me Shit Bag, he'd stop like *that*.' I snap my fingers.

Lockie shoves his hands over his face and I see that he's started biting his nails again. 'I didn't. I'm a dick. I just didn't know how to . . .' He stays there for a while, his hands hiding his face. 'You needed me and I wasn't there for you.'

'Too fucking right, you weren't! Imagine how that was for me. Imagine if you were the one who went through all I've gone through, and all your friends started calling you that nickname and they ignored you and cut you off and were laughing behind your back – not just the girls but the boys too – and . . . I pulled Meathead!' I grimace. 'Oh, I'm really g— Gu-uh!'

'Shit! I'll— Muuum!'

That's the problem with drinking a lot of cordial. It

lubricates everything. It turns the stuff in your stomach into a churning elderflower soup. And it's just so much easier for things to spill out that way. I puke, a ton, into the bin. And it's leaked through the wicker weave, over my cargos and onto Lockie's duvet by the time Mum and Ems get upstairs.

And as they're fussing round me with towels and hustling me through to the family bathroom, my phone rings.

'Hello?' I answer immediately, not ready to hear the news, and feeling generally overwhelmed with my life, but then Mel says, 'He's good. He's out and awake!'

It took some talking on the way home in the car to convince Mum and Dad that my puking on Lockie's bed wasn't an emergency. I guess Chris being rushed to hospital by air ambulance made them paranoid. But I explained, I wasn't in pain like before, just angry. And in explaining why I was angry, I slipped into a bit of a rant about Lockie barely visiting me in hospital – which they knew about – and progressed to his pulling Suriya and instigating the Shit Bag nickname that Meathead spread round the entire school, which they absolutely did *not* know about.

And so . . . yeah.

Now they know that I didn't make up Shit Bag as a nickname because I'm a maudlin masochist.

Mum is livid with Lockie. And she may or may not have told Ems, as yet.

Good luck on explaining that one to your mum, my ex-love!

But despite my cathartic venting to Lockie tonight there's still something important left unsaid. I didn't get to ask him if he saw my stoma through the clear bag in High Dependency. Did he full-on ghost me because he finds my shit bag repellent? Does he find *me* repellent?

Because the really messed-up thing is that I still feel confused about my feelings. I don't think I can trust him anymore. But still, I know him like the back of my hand. And it's hard to just cut your hand off. You tend to be attached to them. Can't do without them. Not without going through some serious pain and loss in the process.

I'm cuddling Winston, my giant fluffy bed partner, snoozing. Turns out puking your guts up in your ex's bedroom does wonders for allowing your bag to stay relatively empty in the morning, resulting in the rare luxury of a lie-in. Silver linings. When my phone gives me need for yesterday's defibrillator. Who's calling me now? Chris! On video. I yank Winston round my back as another pillow, flatten my hair and answer.

And Chris breaks onto my screen with his signature grin. 'Shit Bag!'

In perfect synch I say, 'You're alive!'

'Just . . .' he whispers, because I know those nurses can be weird about phone calls. 'Have you missed me?' he says.

I pout and knock my head from side to side.

'You have, haven't you . . .'

'Maybe. Did you dream about me when you were on the morphine?'

'Still on it, Shit Bag. This conversation is one big dream. Girl of my dreams.'

I scrunch my nose. 'Let's see your wound then?'

His face lights up. Evidently he's well up for a show and tell. He's wearing one of those lovely medical gowns that open at the back and show off your bum. And as he opens it to show me his tummy, I realise that the ties are done up at the front. And my mind is completely and utterly blown because I suddenly remember Chris has no need whatsoever to have the opening of a surgical gown at the back ever again. Because his bumhole is now a hole on his stomach. And his back door has been closed. Permanently.

This throws me, so I don't focus on what he's showing me immediately. And then I do focus. And I realise he's pointing to his stoma through a clear ostomy bag. The exact same kind of clear bag Lockie would've seen my new ostomy through when I was in High Dependency. And as I listen and nod and watch as Chris's long fingers point and gesticulate and he describes how the surgeon told him the way he'd manipulated inside Chris's gut to untwist it, to save him from more invasive surgery, to save him from that excruciating pain that had me so worried I'd never see him again, I have a revelation.

Last night I asked Lockie to consider what it would be like if the situation was reversed and *he'd* got the ostomy, that nickname, and then *I'd* rejected him. But I know categorically that it wouldn't have played out like it has, if I'd seen in through Lockie's clear bag. Even if I was freaked out initially. Hadn't wanted to look at his stoma again. I wouldn't have treated him like he's treated me. I'd have hidden my squeamishness from him. I'd have sucked it up! I'd NEVER abandon him like he has me. Because, our relationship history aside, we're friends. And real friends don't do that.

In this moment, I decide Lockie's let me down irredeemably. And it's time to cut him loose.

Mum and me go away for a few days to stay with my cousins in Ireland before school starts. I think she's feeling bad about what happened with Lockie and the Shit Bag nickname. She's conflicted though, because it's her best mate and her good friends' kids who caused it all (Mum and Dad are friends with Meathead's parents too). So I think she's going to have a word in her own way rather than go in heavy via school for bullying.

I don't really care if the boys are pissed off that I told her. They told everyone at school my name's Shit Bag! Who's the bigger dickheads in that scenario?

CHAPTER 27

'Nervous?' Dad says, nodding at the piece of toast I've shredded into bread confetti.

'I'm trying to eat less processed carbs now, remember?' I say.

'I remember. What did the omelette do wrong?'

I drop my fork with a clatter. 'I'm not hungry.'

'Want me to call school, see if you can start tomorrow instead?' he says.

I drum my fingers on the kitchen table and rattle my head quickly before I can change my mind.

'We'll leave in ten minutes then.' Dad lifts his mug and sinks back into his iPad.

I scrape my chair back and traipse upstairs.

In my room, I curl up on my bed. My eyes are open but it's all going on inside my head. I'm about to walk into school wearing an ostomy bag. On my own. Without the moral support of my friends. Worse, with everyone in school knowing I have a bag.

And calling me Shit Bag.

Can't even fathom how bad it would be if it fell off in class like it did at camp!

Who can I ask for help? I suppose Morven's the obvious one. The only one. She'll go get the school nurse if something really bad happens. But still, she can't really understand what it's like being locked in that loo. How I empty my bag, or make sure it's wiped clean. How much quicker it is than going to the loo normally. In and out. Done. As long as nothing comes *undone*. What do I do if that happens? Morven *will* go get the nurse. I know Ems and John would want Lockie to do the same, but that sure ain't happening now.

Is it really the entire school calling me Shit Bag? Or is it just Meathead's cronies? I can't find that meme anymore to be able to see how many likes it's running at.

'Five minutes, Freya!'

Bollocks. 'Okay!'

I mobilise. Grab my school bag and take out the make-up case Mum got free with Christmas perfume, to check its contents again. I've got enough emergency kit to do two full bag changes. If my bag falls off a third time, however, I'm in a mess, but not completely shafted. I've also got emergency electrical tape – not unlike the

Batman duct tape Jessica had but this stuff is without logo and the plastic's slightly stretchier. Chris recommended it. The Second Rows in his rugby team use it to tape friction bandages to their thighs – so their teammates have something to hold onto when they lift them in the rugby line-out (you learn something new every day). Soon after Chris got his bag, he had a mishap while watching his teammates play. He hadn't brought any spare kit and his flange was peeling off. He managed to get some electrical tape off one of the boys during half-time and wrapped it all around his stomach to hold the flange in place – and it worked a treat. The versatility of tape! I've got two full rolls: yellow and green stripes, and blue.

In the bathroom I empty my bag again even though it doesn't really need emptied. And I down two more loperamide.

'Are you coming?'

'Yes!'

'I'll see you at the end of the day, yeah?' I say to Dad when he parks up outside school.

'Uh? Is that the plan? I thought you'd be getting the train like normal?' Dad says.

'I told you, I'll probably be knackered by lunchtime.'

'Right. Okay, yes then. If I can't be here your mum will be.'

'Okay . . .' I don't sound convinced, because I'm not. I can't believe they've forgotten they're picking me up. I really don't want to have to get myself home tonight. I feel like today's going to be traumatic enough.

I get out of the 4x4 and end up having to shove the door shut twice to get it to click properly. And there was me telling Chris I feel fit enough to play hockey after my week at camp. Luckily, I've had second thoughts. Hockey can wait. I'll have more than enough to be getting on with in a normal school day.

I put my head down, tuck my bag into my side and walk up the street towards the school gates. I finally got my hair trimmed and shaped short last week, after so much of the longer stuff came out, so maybe no one will recognise me anyway. And my first day back will pass unnoticed and uneventful.

My stoma moved on the drive here so first I go to the accessible loo beside the Head's office – no one will dare call me Shit Bag within her hearing range – and empty my bag. I spray my lemon air freshener, wash up and swallow a peppermint oil capsule Mel recommended. The peppermint reduces wind in your gut but, even better, it makes my poo smell minty fresh – really! – which will make sharing loos slightly less traumatic for both me and the next cubicle visitor.

I walk down the corridor, past teachers nodding and smiling that good-old-sympathy-smile that all adults and Morven seem to reserve for me. I think that's what I'm going to miss most about Camp Kill Me Now. No one smiled sadly and sympathetically at me. They just thought I was that annoying, angry girl who insisted on calling herself Shit Bag. Except for Henners. He always looked at me like I was some sort of leader. Like a little Minion with eyes of wonder and amazement. I miss Henners. Wonder what he's doing today. Hope he's playing at school and has a gang of friends ready to share their Fruit Shoots with him.

I pause outside the door of the Sixth Form common room and peer through the glass. It doesn't seem too busy. Looks like there are a couple of vending machines over on the left wall. I could just go straight there. Where's my purse? Bottom of my bag. I'll have to set my bag down on a chair to get the purse out. That would mean I could have a rest first too. Get strength into my shaky, nervous legs before class. Can't see any of my crowd. Wish I'd said yes to Morven when she offered to meet me at the school gates.

'Oh! Hi, Freya! How are you?'

'Uh – hi, Sarah!'

Sarah Matheson – Lowettsons Girls' First XI Hockey Captain. U18 Scotland hockey and lacrosse teams. 'You coming in?'

'Eh, yeah.' I step back and she pushes the door in and walks ahead to hold it open for me so I don't even have to lift a finger.

'You're looking really well!' she says brightly, letting the door shut.

'Thanks.' I follow her across the open expanse of the common room, keeping my eyes fixed on her relaxed, tanned face.

'Are you back for good now?'

'Eh . . . yeah. Think so.'

'Nice. Sorry you missed Portugal. Any chance of you back playing soon?'

I grimace briefly. 'Probably not for a while. I . . . uh. Well, maybe. Might need another operation first.'

'Damn. That's shit.'

I smile awkwardly. I'm not sure how much to share. It was easy at camp. They told you to spill your guts from the start. And that way, when you accidentally spilled your guts on a beach during a team-building exercise they weren't fazed. 'Yeah . . . It's pretty shit that I missed the trip and . . .' I take a second to scan my horizons. Sarah's about to wrap this convo up – I can feel it – and I need to work out where I'm going next.

Otherwise I'm going to be stranded at sea in the middle of this common room surrounded by circling sharks sixth-sensing my injury in the water, smelling my fear, ready to bite me. And then I spot them, near the back of the room on beanbags and a sofa. All of them. Morven and Suriya, with a load of the hockey team, and behind them Lockie, Meathead and Shawsie and a load of other rugby boys. I refocus on Sarah. I can't remember what I was saying.

'Yeah . . . but you could pick it up quick enough,' she says, like I'm not a scatterbrained moron who can't keep her focus on the ball. 'You know what these training trips are like. Half the team just piss about and end up getting drunk on the beach or cycle into a wall and break their arm like Olly Nichols!'

'He didn't?!'

She quirks a grin and nods. 'Idiot.'

I feel a glow spread across the back of my head and through my body. It's like when you press the morphine pump and you're waiting for it to soften the edges and then you realise it's blurring. But this time, it's . . . pleasure. Happiness for being made part of it. I don't think Sarah has any idea how that just made me feel after everything I've been through lately. How I felt walking up the driveway. Maybe I'm not quite as separate from all of this as I thought I was?

'Anyway,' she says, 'good to see you back. I can speak to Ms Jarvis for you when you're ready to play. We're missing you on the Left.' And then she does something so unexpected that I just stand there stunned afterwards. She hugs me. A proper tight-squeeze hug. The sort of hug that I've been missing because everyone else has barely touched me since my collapse because I might break. Muscles, tendons and ligaments clenching and conveying a power into my body. And off she goes to sit at one of the study desks over by the windows, like she has things to do other than mucking around and chatting.

I scan the room quickly again. Look back for a moment to the beanbags and sofa, regret it instantly when I make eye contact with Suriya, who in one brief second looks almost hopeful and happy to see me, waves even.

And not knowing how to handle this. Her. The others. Can I overlook everything that's happened and just go back to my old life? Forgive and forget and forge forward (as much as I can without my bowel and this bag of shit on my belly)? I wave back.

Why? Why did I wave?

I turn and head for the exit. And walk out into fresh air and freedom.

I had planned on calling Chris for a debrief at morning break – he's still at home in Perth recuperating and won't be in Edinburgh until Sunday night to start term at Merchants – but the school nurse suggests I have a lie-down when I check in with her and I end up having a nap. She lets me sleep on, and that makes me late for double art. But at least I'm rejuvenated enough to endure our life drawing class of an old lady in cowboy boots, fringed shirt and cowboy hat, which reminds me of Morven's sixteenth birthday – another lifetime ago.

The routine of school feels foreign but at the same time comforting. Familiar. Going through the motions of a normal life. Reconnecting. Even if I don't feel entirely normal underneath. Underneath this loose school skirt that's tenting – because I'm still thinner than my norm – over my bag, which is ready to be emptied again.

Worried that walking into the dining room late for lunch will put a bullseye on my head, I ask Mr Andrews to excuse me from art class early *because of my situation*.

The loo in the art block is an accessible loo, thankfully, so I easily manage to get everything emptied and washed up and check the flange is still fully stuck in place. I can say flange without even flinching now. Even in the real world! FLANGE!

Flat-stomach profile resumed. The school bell rings just as I'm drying my hands.

'Frey, can we talk?' Suriya blurts in my face as soon as I open the door. And my spirit leaves my body.

'Jeez–us!' I say, grasping my chest and slamming the loo door behind me in one.

'Sorry. I knew you had art. I— We should talk . . .'

'I need to get to lunch,' I say. Did I spray the Poo Pourri? I can't remember. I must've. It smells like lemon up my nose. And mint. Thank God for the peppermint capsules. Still, can she smell it? Like the air when you pass a sewage plant. I'm probably immune to how bad it is by now. It's probably flooding the hall. I walk quickly towards the swing doors, trying to lead Suriya away like the Pied Piper of Stinky Town. 'Talk and walk if you want,' I mumble over my shoulder.

'I'm sorry, Frey!' she babbles. 'I don't know what else to say. I don't know what happened. But it's all over. We're not together . . .'

I pause outside on the steps to the main school building. 'I know.'

'You know?'

'Lockie told me.'

'Lockie . . . told you?'

'Of course.'

I watch the outline of Suriya's tongue do a strange circuit round the inside of her mouth as she blinks. She's thinking. Dangerous for someone like her. 'It wasn't just me, Freya. You should blame him too.'

I'm not admitting I agree with her. That I think they're as bad as each other. That I even think Morven should be included in the list of bad guys and gals because she *and* Suriya didn't stand up for me to Meathead et al. So I say instead, 'You were my best friend, Suriya. There're rules.'

'But you weren't his girlfriend anymore.'

'You're right. And you didn't even make it that far.' I can see she doesn't get what I'm saying so I make it brutally clear. 'You didn't even make it as far as being his girlfriend. I hope a few weeks of Lockie were worth losing your best friend over.' I shrug my satchel up on my shoulder, tramp up the steps and push in through the heavy panelled doors. There. I've said it.

CHAPTER 28

I've got my lunch and I'm sat hiding behind a particularly distracting hair-flicky glamour gang of Fifth Form girls by the time I see Morven come into the dining room and join Suriya and the big table of Firsts hockey girls.

Seems even the school cooks know about my bag because when I told the lady serving that I'd have spaghetti with meatballs her wary eyes kept flashing towards my stomach like she was expecting, at any moment, my bag would pop up above my waistband and go *peek-a-boo*! I wonder who else is watching me *right now*. Imagining what I'm packing. This is such a fucked-up situation. There's a girl at the centre of the Fifth Form Glamazons throwing me sneers.

Morven's suddenly standing opposite me. 'Hi,' she says. 'I like your hair.'

'Thanks.' So much for my incognito strategy.

'How was this morning? I planned on seeing you first thing and getting one of the boys to help carry your bag for you. Are you feeling okay? You're not feeling queasy or anything?'

I blink. Aware of the younger girls beside us. And the fact that Morven's babying me. Treating me again like I'm so delicate that getting through a normal day at school will break me. I'm just that fragile.

'Why would I feel queasy?'

'Um, Lockie said you were sick at his house.' She looks over to the food counters and I see Lockie getting his lunch there. The sight of him twists my stomach. At the loss of everything that's normal, including him.

Morven continues, 'And you were sick in hospital. I thought that was part of what happens?'

To be fair, she's right. I have been a bit of a puker lately. 'Well, better out than in!' I pull the sarcastic jokey face Chris and me vibed off all camp, but Morven just sits down on the bench opposite, looking concerned.

I get this weird force-field sensation and look over to the glamour girls, and the one in the middle's watching us. 'We're being watched,' I say to Morven, tipping my head to the side.

Morven follows my lead, clocks the girl and narrows her eyes like she's properly going to laser-beam her.

I frown. 'What's going on?' I murmur.

'Nothing,' Morven says. 'Anyway, why are you sitting here?'

'I'm eating my lunch, obvs.'

'Come sit with everyone else.'

'I'm not in the team anymore, remember.'

Morven pulls a face. 'Is it because of the thing with Suriya?'

Is it? Probably not. Or maybe not only her. I know I just spewed all that crap to Suriya at the art block about Lockie. But now it's purged, I feel like that's over. Chris and me are vibing. And I can't wait for him to come back to Edinburgh so we can meet and see whether it'll turn into anything legitimately like a relationship. But rejoining the gang right now, today?

'Maybe tomorrow,' I say.

Morven glances at the younger girls as she gets up off the bench. 'Okay. I need to get some lunch. Why don't you come over and say hi to everyone when you've finished.'

I nod. But I think I might go for a walk outside before afternoon classes in the hope that I can get my rumbling guts to let off steam – i.e. fart. Because my joke about 'better out than in' feels a little too close to reality now that I can feel my guts churning with lunch, and without a sphincter to keep all of that in, double maths could be *Thundery With the Chance of Meatballs*!

* * *

My afternoon goes by uneventfully. Lockie sits at the back of our maths class and I sit near the middle of the room. He's doodling in his ring binder when I walk in, so we don't make eye contact. After my walk round the games pitches, my tummy keeps relatively quiet up until the last half-hour of class. When I feel this rolling, looming bubble of wind start to move through my gut. But instead of panicking, and drawing attention to myself by leaving the room, I just prod my fingers through my clothes against the opening of my stoma and sit there with it plugged – just like the Little Dutch Boy who plugged the leaking hole in the dyke with his finger – until the bell and the end of class when everyone clatters and scrapes their chairs back in a racket and I move my hand away from my stoma to let rip.

With real relief that I made it through my first day back and it wasn't as bad as I'd imagined it would be, I go empty my barely filled bag for the fifth time today. School's a piece of piss to manage an ostomy compared with canyoning down a mountain river with no loo in sight!

To be fair, that wasn't difficult with an ostomy either.

And once I'm done, I head out to text Dad asking where he's collecting me from and discover there's already a message from Mum.

Mum: Can't get to school in time for pick up. Lockie's going to come home with you on the train. I'll collect you from theirs. It's about time he stepped up and helped you. You'll be fine! And just so you know – Ems spoke to him about the Shit Bag bullying.

Fuck!

I'm waiting by the art-block steps for Lockie, when Morven comes out of the main school doors. 'Oh, hey!' she says.

I look immediately past her to see if Suriya's there. If Lockie's on his way I can't deal with everyone together in one place. That's going to end today on a sour note and I'm just not up to it emotionally. But she's not there.

'Hi!' I say, upbeat, realising I'm genuinely glad to see Morven. This is just like old times. Me, Morven and Lockie and . . . not Suriya . . .

'You okay?'

'Great, thanks.'

'You getting home okay?'

'I'm sorted, thanks.'

'I meant to ask earlier, but I didn't want to mention him

while those little bitches were eavesdropping. How's it been with Lockie today? You just had maths, didn't you?'

'Yeah. It was fine. We didn't sit together, if that's what you're asking.' I can't help but be a little frosty. I see Lockie heading towards us from the sports hall. He waves. I wave briefly. And focus back on Morven, nodding to the side. 'Speaking of the devil. He's checking I get home safe. Apparently I need a chaperone these days.'

Morven's face lights up like a 5000-lumen LED.

'It's *not* that, Morven.'

Her whole face – mouth, eyebrows, forehead – are independently partying.

I roll my eyes at her. I haven't told her my private business yet. She doesn't know about Chris.

Morven has barely pulled it together by the time Lockie's with us. 'Hi, Lockie!' she says, beaming.

'Hi, Morven,' he sing-songs back, making me concerned where *his* head's at too. 'You okay?' he says, turning to me.

I bite my bottom lip and nod.

'I've got to leave Brycey's boots in the common room first,' Lockie says, waving them at me, once Morven's left us 'to it'. 'I'll leave this here.' He kicks his school bag closer to the bush I'm standing beside.

'Yeah, sure.'

He takes the stone steps two at a time and disappears inside.

I swing my feet side to side, shifting my weight from foot to foot, as I flick through my phone. I go into my messages from Chris and try to word something that sounds suitably amusing about how my day's been.

A group of younger girls come down the steps, giggling. 'There's no way he's back with her now. Absolutely rotten!'

'Ugh!'

I look up and watch them turn towards me to head along the path. I realise it's the Fifth Form girls from my table at lunch. They're all suddenly silent. I make eye contact with the one who was looking at me. She locks on, bold as you like, and doesn't let go until they've passed. I watch her back. A few more paces away they snort and burst out laughing, all of them. One of the girls looks over her shoulder. Says something as she turns back. And they squeal and run.

'Sorry!' Lockie reappears. 'You ready to go?'

I nod.

'Let me get that,' Lockie says, reaching for my satchel.

'I'm fine.'

'Freya.'

'Lockie, you're not my boyfriend anymore.'

'If I don't carry your bag, Frey, I'm dead.'

Knowing his mum probably flayed strips off him for Shit Bag, I mutter, 'Fine,' and hand over my satchel.

'Let's get the bus to Haymarket.'

'I can walk, Lockie.'

He shrugs at me, opening out his palms as if he has no choice. Clearly Ems and John have him under strict warnings.

I roll my eyes and make a *growl* sound in my throat. 'Maybe you should carry me too.'

He laughs all too easily, like we're pals again, and says, 'Wouldn't be the first time I've had to do that.' He swings both bags over his shoulder and walks on through the school gates. There's something about Lockie's broad shoulder under his white shirt and my little satchel swinging dinkily from it that hits me in the gut. I watch the easy rhythm of my school bag as it moves with his body.

It makes me want to bend my knees, lie down on the warm Tarmac and cry.

But I don't. Because I haven't forgotten about Lockie and Suriya. So I shout after him, 'It would be the last time you do that though!'

Kids from other years glance over their shoulders at me. Lockie doesn't. He keeps on walking. Maybe he didn't hear me. Is his back tense? Why did I need to shout that?

He's leaning against the metal bench in the bus shelter, totally focused on his phone, when I catch him up. Most of the crowd are from younger years and are standing a respectful distance away. I push into the narrow space between Lockie and some girl, and suddenly I realise it's the brazen Glamazon who's been haunting me all day. She doesn't budge and I have to death-stare her. There's a moment when she seems to think she can challenge me, then she gives in. But not without a curl of her lip and a disgusted, nose-scrunching sniff as if she can smell something foul off me and then mimes retching. Her mates, standing over by the timetable sign, snort and piss themselves laughing and Bitch Girl saunters over to them, waving her hand like a fan to waft away my stench.

I planned to apologise to Lockie but I can't say anything now. I need . . . I need to walk. I grab his arm and pull.

'Frey? We have to get the bus. What?' He glances over his shoulder. 'What's wrong?'

'Nothing. Just, please can we walk?'

'If you want. But if you get tired, we'll get the bus, okay?'

I keep marching, just out of Lockie's reach so he can't see that I'm crying. In fact . . . this is bad. I'm really crying. I need to – RUN.

I keep running.

And Lockie runs with me. I don't stop until I pass the black Tardis police box, at the end of West Coates. And only then because a coach is turning left for the hotel on the corner and blocking our path and I'm close to boaking up my lungs. I glance over my shoulder urgently and see that the number 12 bus is about to catch us up. So instead of letting those girls in the double-decker pass by and see me upset, I take a left and walk up the side of the road. Lockie follows. We're going the wrong way. The train station is another four hundred metres along the main road. But now I've seen that Fifth Form girl snuggled up beside him at the bus stop, I remember she gets the same train as Lockie. I can't sit on the train with them laughing at me.

I skirt the black railings enclosing the private garden for the tenement houses, past the steps down to the walkway along the river and hang a right onto Douglas Crescent. I like it here. The ancient, soot-tinged Georgian houses overlook another narrow tree-flanked garden. It's cut off from the general public by black spiked railings. Anyone savvy about Edinburgh knows not to try and climb the railings – Lockie will vouch for that. He and Meathead were pissed one night and decided to break into a similar, grander garden in the New Town. Lockie ended up with a spike through his boot into his foot. He missed half the rugby season because of it. Anyway, there are now metal bicycle-parking bunkers on the side of the road. And they're a brilliant stepping stone into the garden.

I give Lockie the eye and he nods, knowing what I'm planning. He drops our bags and links his hands so I can step up, and he boosts me onto the top of the box. I jump off onto the other side of the railings. I have to close my eyes for a moment and deal with the shooting pain up my shins – I haven't really jumped like that since I had my operation. I walk away, trying to ignore the ache. When our school bags and Lockie are over the fence we walk to a bench tucked into the trees and sit. We've been here many times before. It's comforting to be here again. Like everything in life is normal and none of the last few months have happened.

Except, of course, I can feel my bag under my skirt and there's a tiny bit of warmth like it's a perpetually renewing warm-water bottle. Trust me to spoil the moment thinking about my bag and shit. But then that's the point. It's all because of this bag and shit. That's why we're here. Because of that girl and her friends, and them knowing about my shit bag. I just remembered she's called Imogen.

'You alright?' Lockie says.

My eyes are probably red and puffy from crying. 'Yeah – fine.'

Lockie takes out his phone and messages someone. And then puts it away. 'Let's not tell Mum and Dad about the running. Okay?' he says.

I nod. 'Sorry about earlier – when I said it would be the last time you carried me.'

'S'alright. I'm sorry too, Frey. About . . . everything.'

I nod briefly. 'Can we just chill here for a bit?'

'Sure.'

Birdsong filters up from the trees behind us, down by the river's walkway. I pick out wood pigeons among the racket and it reminds me of when Lockie and me thought their calls were cuckoos. 'Remember when we recorded the pigeons to make a cuckoo clock?'

He's biting his bottom lip and smiles through it at the memory. 'You mean the coo clock.'

'Yeah.' This makes me laugh.

And he laughs too.

This isn't what I planned. It's not that easy. We're not back to normal. You don't get to just smile at me and I melt. 'You've really hurt me,' I say.

His smile drops and he nods, picking at the black paint – layers and layers built up over a century – on the bench's slatted seat. This is our relationship. Too many layers. Too many scratches and wounds and broken flecks, covered over and disguised by a glossy top coat. But the flaws are still visible if you look closely.

'I need you to be honest with me,' I say.

'Course,' he says, his blue eyes staring into my soul.

'Did you stop coming to see me . . .' I have to take a breath before I finally get it out, 'because you saw my gut through my bag in High Dependency?'

He moves when my words hit him. And as I recognise what that shift means – imperceptibly minor if I wasn't waiting for it – the impact rebounds, gut-punching me.

I knew it!

I get up and walk away into the trees. My lungs are doing that gasping thing they do when the air is dry and ten below zero. But worse, I realise, the tree I've come to, literally hugging for comfort, is the one we scratched our initials in years ago.

Lockie comes forward and I hold my finger up, warning him off.

'It was a shock, Frey. I couldn't face you after that. That time Mum and Dad forced me to come see you. I felt so bad—'

Forced me to come see you. 'Shut up! Shut up, Lockie—!' I can't be sick again. This constant retching. Why's every physical reaction going for my gut? And my heart . . .

He's crying now. Clenching his hands, opening them, pleading. He wants to hug me, but he knows I'll deck him if he dares touch me uninvited. He rubs his mouth and watches, waiting for me to say I forgive him.

And I dissolve in floods, letting months of fear, revulsion and disgust at myself slip out. Allowing him to wrap me up finally, shielding me from all the horrible reality of what I've been through alone.

Wiping away tears, kissing my cheeks, until he's kissing my mouth and I'm lost in my past.

CHAPTER 29

I wake just after six thirty a.m. with my bag full of air. I stumble to the loo and I'm back in bed in a blur. I was only up twice through last night. That's got to be a record.

It was probably the dive in hormones after yesterday's adrenaline. Worrying about what would happen with my bag and the nickname, and then what *actually happened* with Lockie.

I must have fallen back to sleep because my alarm wakes me again twenty minutes later. Delaying dragging myself out of bed, I check my phone.

Chris: Morning, Shit Bag!

Chris: Are you awake?

Biting the skin around my nails, I look at both messages. I know Chris and I haven't put a label on anything. That we've literally kissed a few times and that was two weeks ago now. We even said we'd see how it goes when we're both back in Edinburgh. But still. What happened yesterday with Lockie is shit. On my part.

Obviously it wasn't planned. It just happened.

I don't know . . . I'm confused. As much as my head is screaming at me to walk away from Lockie and start running, sprinting, towards Chris. That's easier said than done. Especially when Lockie will be there, every day, at school. And we have all this history. Baggage too. But still. I have to get my head straight before I say anything to Chris about it. Because Lockie's kiss was a surprise. Painful, even. But it was also warm. Comforting. Safe. Desperate. A thrill. And a total head-fuck!

So what do I do?

Block it out? Yesterday is yesterday. And today is a new day?

I type to Chris:

Me: Morning!

Biting my bottom lip, I wait.
Just seconds.

Chris: Finally! I've got news.

Me: What? Tell me!

Chris: It's not health-related, don't worry. I'm coming to Edinburgh early! Fancy meeting me on Friday after school?

Me: Friday – as in tomorrow?????

Chris: Ha! Yes, tomorrow!!!!!!!!!!!!

I touch my hair self-consciously and look down the front of my pyjama top.

Chris: Well? Don't leave me hanging, Shit Bag! Don't make me video-call you just so that I can see you in your PJs. In fact I've missed the early morning PJ action . . .

My phone lights up with a video-call from him. I press Accept and I'm laughing when I see his wide grin fill the screen. 'What's on your PJs today, Shit Bag?' he says.

I look down as if I haven't just literally looked there. 'They're very appropriate. I can get you a pair for Christmas if you want?'

'What is it?' he squints, his eye looming to the camera comedically.

I move the camera down, and pull the top straight so he can see only fabric and not that ridiculously named bit of flesh, my décolletage. But he's silent so I guess he still can't see it.

'Winnie the Pooh! Want a pair?'

He yawns and smiles. 'Definitely! Although Tigger's my spirit animal. Get me a Tigger pair for Christmas.' He shifts onto his side, so I get a flash of his bare brown shoulder and of a white pillow. He's in bed too. 'So tell me more about how yesterday went,' he says.

Yesterday. *Yesterday I kissed my ex . . . And today is a new day.* 'School was okay . . .' I'm thinking about the rest of Chris's torso. 'What are *you* wearing?' I blurt.

He throws his head back, laughing at me.

Couldn't help it. 'I mean, are *you* wearing pyjamas?' I bury my mouth below the lapel of my pyjamas to try and hide my smirk.

'Want to see what I'm wearing?'

'Yes! You are wearing something, aren't you?'

'Yeah, Shit Bag. Not a fan of having my bag loose when I'm sleeping. That's a recipe for disaster.' He waves his hand, signalling we don't need to discuss the times he's had a leak through the night. 'So no,' he says, 'I don't sleep naked,' looking through the phone at me with those deep-sea eyes.

Gah. He's got my tummy twisting.

'If that's what you were wondering?' he adds.

'Well, no,' I say, deadpan. 'I was just wanting to see your kecks in all honesty.'

I get the reaction I want and he knocks his head back against his pillow, laughing again. I have an overwhelming urge to kiss him on his throat. But I snuggle down under Winston's giant teddy-bear arm instead so I can imagine Chris is here hugging me.

'Here you go, Shit Bag.' The phone image pans round erratically and I get a flash of his stomach, then his hip, and his ostomy bag tucked into the waistband of his boxers. They're grey Calvin Klein.

His face reappears. 'Verdict?'

'Meh. Bit basic.'

'Basic? The cheek of you! I'll give you basic.'

I hide inside my pyjama top again, and we fall into one of those slightly awkward tumbleweed moments when you don't know what to say because you're too busy thinking about *other* things. Is he thinking about *other* things?

'So,' he finally says, 'you were telling me about yesterday?'

'Ugh. Was I?'

'Shit Bag?'

'Well, some Fifth Form girls were mean to me but they're harmless.'

'What? Want me to come flirt with them and then kiss you in front of them?'

'YES, PLEASE!'

'Done. So tomorrow Mum's helping my godmother do the food for her birthday party at the weekend. I need *you* to save me from peeling langoustines all day?' He flutters his eyelashes. 'Pretty please!'

'We're both doing charitable work saving each other. What's there to discuss? It's a date.'

'A date?'

'Figure of speech.'

Chris nods, his lips quirking and twitching at the side like he's fighting one of his grins.

'I think my last class finishes at four.'

'Shall I meet you outside those black gates?'

I nod, fiddling with my lapel to hide my excitement. 'Yup.'

'Now, you promise not to make a scene, Shit Bag? I

know you've missed me. I was on death's door the last time we saw each other in person . . .'

I roll my eyes. 'See you tomorrow, Chris!'

He grins and salutes.

And I hang up and squeal into Winston's fluffy chest.

CHAPTER 30

Soon as I'm through the school gates, I hear, 'Finally!'

I know it's Lockie before I even look. The plinth just inside the entrance is his usual spot to wait for me. I just haven't had that special treatment since . . . before we started arguing at Easter.

He jumps down from the brick pillar and shoulders his bag. 'You good?' he says, taking my satchel from my shoulder and adding it to his load, then leaning in to kiss me.

I back off.

'What?' he says.

'Lockie, about yesterday. It doesn't mean anything. It doesn't change anything. You know that?'

He shrugs. 'Yeah . . . 'Course.'

I nod and squint my lips.

He sighs. 'Morven says I'm to bring you to the common room.'

'Why?'

He doesn't answer.

I look at him. 'Why does she want me in the common room, Lockie?'

'I might've told her we kissed . . .'

'Lockie!'

'What? I was excited. I had to tell someone.'

Fuck. We start walking. He's still carrying my satchel. 'Why were you excited?' I ask just before the sports hall.

'Why do you think?'

'I genuinely have no idea, Lockie.' One of the Fifth Form girls from yesterday is walking towards us – not Imogen.

'Don't say that,' Lockie says.

'Say what?'

'Freya, I wanted us to get back together!'

'Why?'

'Because I love you!'

'Do you though? I'm not trying to be cold, Lockie. I'm being honest. Your behaviour doesn't show me that you love me. No matter what words you use.' I realise as I say this that I'm paraphrasing what Chris said to me that day my bag fell off. '*If someone cheats on you or acts like they don't respect you, then you need to recognise what they're showing you and cut them loose.*'

And I realise this is something I've already learned from Chris. Boundaries. That Lockie – no matter what we've been through, no matter our history, no matter his excuses – has gone multiple steps too far.

'Yeah, but I've explained all that, Freya. I've apologised,' Lockie says, frustrated.

'You have. And now I'm explaining how *I* feel.' I'm abrupt. Snappy. Because now I have a taste of acid in the back of my throat. I've behaved the same way towards Chris when I kissed Lockie yesterday. And Chris is going to cut *me* loose.

I pull Morven aside in the common room and put her straight on the fact there won't be anything more happening between me and Lockie. She humours me but insinuates that it's just a matter of time before our on-again-off-again is . . . on again. I don't ask her if she told Suriya. If she did, then she can rectify that herself. But I agree to join both of them and the hockey team at lunch. There's part of me that's a little nervous to eat lunch alone after yesterday's interaction at the bus stop. But I know it will be relatively chill at lunchtime anyway because the rugby Firsts are away doing some charity thing so they're eating early.

'Freya! How *are* you?' our goalie asks me in the dining room, that way healthy people do to sick people. I've just dumped my bag down beside Morven, who already has her food.

'Good, thanks, Emma. How are *you?*' I say.

'Very well!'

I perch on the bench so I can get up for my food shortly. I'm starving. But I want to hold my spot beside Morven in case it's gone when I come back. I catch Emma's eye again and she smiles at me sympathetically. 'Did you have a good summer, Emma?' I ask.

'Really great, thanks. Went to Bermuda.'

'Wow!'

'And obviously Portugal.'

'Obviously.'

'Hey, Freya!' Sarah says, sliding her tray in opposite. She and Emma have a brief trading of information about their U18 Scotland hockey team trial next week.

And then Emma says, 'It's just so sad that you can't play hockey anymore, Freya. I think she could've trialled this term for the U18s if she hadn't got sick, don't you, Sarah?'

'For sure,' Sarah agrees.

'Oh, but I can . . .' I have an out-of-body moment, unsure whether I really said that out loud.

'What?' Emma says.

'I mean, play school hockey. Right, Sarah?'

'Well, yeah! If you're allowed?'

'I'll get my surgeon to write a letter. Just going to get my lunch.' I move quickly across the dining room for the food-serving counter, so that I don't back out. Hockey! That's decided then . . .

It's a bloke serving me today and thankfully he doesn't do the stomach analysis the lady did yesterday. But he gives me two servings of lasagne with my salad, so I guess I do still look like I need feeding up. And as I'm getting a piece of garlic bread, I hear a shriek and explosion of laughter behind me. That's not unusual considering how large the dining room is so I just get on with my plate and turn to walk back.

But the group of Fifth Form girls from yesterday are standing in a gaggle talking to the nearest table of Fifth Form boys. They're spread out like a barrier in the road, blocking my way. But the fact that several girls then glance at me and *don't* move, I can't help but feel something is going on and I might be the target.

I don't know. Call me paranoid. But my heart's drumming at my throat when I try to ease round behind a girl with long red hair, perhaps the girl I saw this morning when I was with Lockie, and the boy beyond her immediately leans over onto the bench behind to talk to someone, and completely blocks me.

I'm not in the mood for fucking around like this. I know that girl Imogen is in the middle of this crowd. I can feel her. So I just shoulder-barge the redhead and walk back the long way round.

But just as I take the next, free lane between benches, I hear a boy shout, 'SHIT BAG!'

And another. 'SHIT BAAAAG!'

And to top it off, a super-loud wet fart sound – PFFFFFFT – followed by a sigh of relief – 'Ahhhhh!' – rips the air of the dining room.

Someone's actually taken the time to download, or fuck knows, maybe they recorded themselves, and brought in a speaker loud enough to boom across the noisy room, just to humiliate me.

I somehow get to the hockey table, I don't remember how, and fold down between the girls. And all around me there's chaos.

Morven hugs me tight. Suriya's gone. I don't know where. She just got up when I collapsed at the table. The other hockey girls have crowded round me. A couple of Upper Six girls twist out from the bench and, with a flick of hair and exposed wrists as they push up their sleeves, head away from us. In the direction of the Fifth Form girls. If Lockie was here, they wouldn't have dared. Would they? I don't know. Meathead dared . . .

Morven calls out over my head, 'She'll sort it. Yeah. Go

with her. Go for it, they were warned last time. Little twats!'

My heart's exploding out of my body. I'm one big heartbeat.

A gap clears in my view and I see Suriya in the distance leaning over talking to one of the Fifth Form boys. She's so low to his ear that the ends of her long hair are almost in his lap. And despite the distance, I can see how frozen and red-faced he is from here. In fact, all the boys have their heads down, staring at the tabletop. The murmur in the dining room lowers and goes silent as everyone tries to hear what's being said. Except for me. I don't want to hear. I'm okay listening to my heartbeat swish.

And then, transfixed, I can't focus on anything else – anyone else – I watch Suriya stand upright, flick her long dark hair back over her shoulder and stalk through the tables, boys and girls poker-straightening their backs to clear her route to her next target. Imogen and friends. And sure enough, Suriya leans down beside the Fifth Form girl who might think she's so glamorous, but she's got nothing on Suriya, and the whole room is silent, holding their breaths, straining to try and hear Suriya.

But we hear nothing.

Until Imogen gets up and runs from the dining room.

CHAPTER 31

'Freya! We slept in!' Mum screams.

'Mmm?'

Mum opens my door again and bellows, 'School!' and slams it.

'I'm up,' I shout from the landing, slamming the bathroom door behind me. I look like crap. Never mind. Wait? What day is it? Yesterday was . . . Thursday. So today is . . . Bollocks! I meant to change my bag last night so it would be fresh for seeing Chris. And I need a shower. A real one. Not just a jet-wash to my bits. And in half an hour I'm going to be late for school.

But I need a shower.

And to change my bag.

But I'm late.

I turn the shower on anyway, empty my bag in the loo – obviously – peel the bag and flange off and bin them. I have a shower with my stoma exposed for old times' sake. Slather myself in coconut shower gel, coconut shampoo and coconut conditioner. I'm one big coconut. Shave my legs and pits. Pat myself dry. Stick loo roll over my stoma while I sit on the pan cutting out a fresh flange.

'Freya! You ready?' Dad calls outside the bathroom door.

'No! My bag was leaking.' Yep, I'm lying, people. 'Just changing it! I'll have to get to school late!' I sound quite calm, considering I'm shaking with the pressure of rushing this.

I stick the paste around the flange and fit it over my stoma. And then press it onto my stomach and clip the already closed bag on over the flange. I quickly clear away all my gear, rush through to my bedroom – feeling light-headed with the panic – and lie down on my bed, in my towel, to rub product into my hair and rough-dry it while trying not to bend at the waist to allow the stickiness of the flange to adhere to my skin.

'You're really late!' Mum pokes her head round my door.

'I know. But my bag came off.'

'Oh, right. I'm going to have to go. I'm getting a lift into work, but I'll phone and tell school why you're late.'

'Okay. Mum—?'

Her head pops back in. 'What?'

'Me and a few of the girls are going to go see a film after school. That okay?' She doesn't need to know I'm

256

meeting Chris today. Knowing Mum, she'll *accidentally* tell Ems. Who'll then tell Lockie.

'Fine. Yeah,' Mum says. 'Call me at lunchtime. Bye. Sandy! I'll call the school.'

I throw on clean underwear and over-the-knee socks. Least I found this Fourth Form skirt in the back of my wardrobe and it's giving me curves again. I've also discovered a jumper from the same era. The sleeves are too short but if I pull them up at the elbow no one will know and actually as it's so tight it even looks like my boobs have returned to their former glory – though that's probably the magic of the new underwear Mum bought me. Today I've wearing a matching red-and-white gingham set.

'Freya?'

'Just coming! I'll be one minute!' I shout, stepping over a pile of dumped clothes. I stick my feet into my favourite suede slip-ons, grab some perfume and a new lip gloss I ordered, shove them into my satchel and run out the door to the car.

Art first thing has got me contemplating life. And Suriya. I keep thinking about yesterday in the dining room. She was kind of glorious! Like exuding female power. In control. The antithesis of how I deal with things.

Morven wouldn't tell me after, what the history is. But

I have a feeling that Imogen and friends were up to *much more* on the Shit Bag front while I was off school in hospital. And the way Suriya swept straight over to sort it out. Didn't say anything when she came back to the table. Just exchanged a look with Morven.

This time I'm absolutely okay with them not sharing what they know with me. Because, *I know now*, Suriya and Morven have my back.

And in turn, that's got me thinking about Lockie.

Suriya's always liked Lockie – I see that now.

So have I, obviously, but I was lucky enough to have it reciprocated and be in a relationship with him since Primary School. Lucky in the sense that that's what I wanted and I got it. Mostly.

And although Suriya and me can be tough on each other, snippy even, she's put up with years of watching Lockie and my on-and-off car-crash relationship play out before her with good grace. Mostly.

And that's a reflection on her being a classy chick.

But there have been times when she's snapped and told me she doesn't want to hear me moaning about him. That I should let him go be happy with someone else.

If only I'd listened to her, perhaps NONE of this would've happened.

So I want to try and fix things for her. I pull Lockie aside before lunch and attempt to broach the Suriya subject.

Only he turns tetchy and defensive, acting like he's pissed off with her. That he'd *never* pull her! Which I know isn't true because *he did*. So I shut up and resolve to ask Morven's advice – it's been a while since we've had a heart-to-heart and maybe I'm missing something.

Then, unexpectedly, Lockie insists on sitting with me at lunch. Saying, 'Yes. I get it, Freya! We're broken up. You've said that. But no one will dare say anything to you again if I'm sitting with you. The rest of school need to know not to fuck with you.'

The irony of this, coming from Lockie, isn't lost on me.

He even makes Meathead lead the way in, like the world's most hypocritical bodyguard. It's the least Meathead can do, in all honesty, considering he started the whole thing. He hasn't said a word to me since I came back to school. Never mind an apology! But that's probably wise on his part. Lockie may have warned him to keep mute for his own safety – especially after my mum told his mum about the Shit Bag meme.

Once I'm sat with Morven, Lockie goes to get my food so I don't have to stand at the counter. I let him serve me. He owes me that. Perhaps he really believes he's protecting me. He's not. He's symbolically pissing on my leg like a territorial dog. 'She's mine, you lot! Fuck with her, you fuck with me.'

I'm kind of numb to it. Done with it. Done with him.

I eat and barely focus on anyone beyond our immediate group. Emma and Sarah tell the squad that I've decided to trial for the hockey team and that gets everyone buoyed up on my behalf. Even Suriya tells me she's proud of me and wishes me luck. This makes me happy.

Lockie, on the flip side, seems concerned for my safety and insists Mum and Dad can't possibly think it's okay.

I say nothing. Just smile. And mentally put another cross in the Lockie column. And a tick below Chris.

By the end of lunch, my nerves are rising. I'm meeting Chris in three and a half hours and I haven't told Morven or Lockie, or the others, that I'm not going to head into town with them after school – they're all going for the usual Friday burgers.

I break the news when we're mooching about in the common room before afternoon classes. 'I forgot to say earlier . . . I'm meeting a friend from camp after school. They're down from Perth for a family thing so we've arranged to catch up.'

'Oh yeah?' Morven says. 'She can come with us if you want? It would be nice to meet some of your friends from camp. You've not told me anything about how it went yet.'

'I will do. Maybe later,' I say, turning a strained smile on her. I'll have to tell Morven about Chris another day when Lockie's not around. 'But it would be good to just talk with my friend. About our bags, you know . . . ?'

Lockie looks surprised when I mention my friend's bag, as if he thought I was the only one.

'She's got one too?' Morven says. 'Wow, Freya! That's so positive. Is she our age? Can we meet her?'

I flinch. 'A year older than us. Chris— Mel's got a permanent bag. And helped me deal with mine.'

I'm going straight to hell.

'Chrismel? That's an unusual name,' Morven says.

'Yeah! It is, isn't it!'

Take me now.

No, really, Satan. I'm ready.

I fidget through double maths so much that Lockie thinks I'm not well. This is confirmed when I take my satchel with me and leave class to go to the loo. But really I'm going to check my make-up and hair, down some marshmallows and – most importantly – message Chris.

> **Me:** Hey, I'm thinking it's easier to meet the opposite side of school. That way we can go straight into town. Shall we meet just outside the Modern Art Gallery at 4.15 p.m.? SBx

I've worked out I need to get off school property quicker than anyone else. Especially before the others have met in the common room after class. I don't know what I was thinking, arranging to meet Chris at the gates.

This is a literal shit show.

I fucked up earlier, massively. Yes, Chris is obviously a boy. And technically I didn't use female pronouns, and I didn't correct Morven when she wrongly presumed. But there's worse. If any of the boys see Chris they'll recognise him from rugby.

They cannot see me with him.

When the bell goes, Lockie waves me off.

I'm out the door, along the corridor and out into the afternoon sun. I speed-walk towards the games pitches and open my phone to check Chris's reply to the message I sent him over forty minutes ago.

There's a big red exclamation mark beside my message. *FLANGE!* It failed to send.

I turn and run back towards the main driveway.

Chris is leaning against the railings wearing aviators, dark jeans and a grey T-shirt, with his phone against his ear. This is the first time I've seen him out of sports gear.

'Hey!'

'Ah, here you are! Hi!' He pushes off from the fence.

Sunglasses off, his arms wind round me, pulling me close to him. In this unexpected moment of wrapped stillness, I exhale. Breathe.

And when he lets me go, I miss him already.

He grins down at me. 'Cool hair!'

'You've seen it on video.' I shove my fingers into it and grip a handful self-consciously.

'It looks even better in real life.'

'You think?' I can feel myself blushing. I need to get this jumper off. It's too warm today for jumpers and running. '*You* look really well,' I say, meaning it.

He looks bigger – maybe broader – than the last time I saw him in person. Who am I kidding with my low-key *he looks bigger*? The boy looks fucking beautiful, people! I can't believe he's here! 'How's your hernia?' I ask.

'Healing remarkably quickly according to the doc.'

'Yeah?' I beam. 'That's good.'

'It certainly is.' Chris nods his head a bit.

I haven't a clue what to say next.

'You're looking great,' Chris manages.

'You think?' I check out my own body, trying to see it with fresh eyes. 'I feel good. Still get tired.' When I look up, I collide with his eyes.

'Want to get out of here?'

'Definitely.'

I notice he cradles his stomach when he tucks his

sunglasses in at the neck of his T-shirt. 'So what's the news, Shit Bag? What've you been up to since I saw you last – in your Winnie the Pooh PJs?'

'Uh, actually, why don't we get the bus into town? It'll be quicker.' I walk through the gates and head down the hill, trying to draw him away from school.

'Shit Bag! Hello? Where are you going? I thought I'd be getting a *hello, I'm glad you're alive* kiss?'

Yes, I want one of those too! I stop on the pavement and lean back against the adjacent wall.

He catches me up. 'Hello . . .' he says, grinning, his tongue prodded against his teeth in a cheeky way.

'Hello,' I say, but I can't help myself and glance nervously up towards the gates. There are kids streaming out of school now. 'Could we . . . maybe hold the *hello* kiss until we're somewhere more private?' I ask.

Chris looks over his shoulder and nods. 'Yeah. Understood. Come on, Shit Bag.' And he kisses the top of my head, lays his arm across my shoulder, hugging me to his side, and kisses me once more. 'Want me to carry that cute little bag of yours?' he asks.

'No. I'm good,' I say leaning into him.

We walk down the hill towards the bus stop, wrapped together as one.

At the bus stop I have a brief and fleeting memory of Imogen and her gang a couple of days ago, and then we get on the bus and they're forgotten. Irrelevant. We go to the top deck. Chris slides in first so that I can lean against him. 'Okay, you were telling me your news. What've you been up to?'

And I remember. *What I've done.* I have to tell him. As soon as we're off this bus. Once we're in private.

I focus on the positives and say, 'I've decided to trial for the hockey team.'

'You have?' He hugs me. 'When? When's the big occasion happening?'

'Monday.'

'Monday! Well, you've worked hard. You're looking fit.'

'Thank you.'

He laughs. 'Want any tips? Or are you feeling in control of the situation?'

'Tips, please,' I say, snuggling into him with a grin.

We're in Princes Street Gardens on the bank when he finally tries to kiss me.

I stop him. 'I need to talk to you about something first.' I tuck my feet up under me and grasp my shoeless toes.

'That sounds ominous. What's up?' He's still grinning.

'Um . . . Something happened . . .'

'You're starting to freak me out a bit, Shit Bag. What's going on?'

I puff my cheeks. 'My ex. We kissed.'

'Right . . .' It's like the north-east wind's blown in from the Firth of Forth.

'Didn't he pull your friend, and give you Shit Bag?'

'And ghosted me after seeing my stoma.' I sigh. 'Yes.'

'I can see why you'd kiss the guy,' Chris says.

The minutest hint of dry humour in his voice makes me grimace, thinking how easy it's been between us until now. But I allow my eyes to meet his. They're cold uncharted waters now.

'Well, this isn't how I thought today would end up,' he says.

I sigh again. 'Nor me.'

'Yeah, I don't know what this is.' He gets to his feet.

'Chris. It's not . . .' It doesn't feel right to tell him that there's nothing between Lockie and me. It sounds cheap. I *feel* cheap.

'When did this happen?'

'Wednesday.'

'We spoke yesterday morning. You didn't think to tell me then?'

'I wanted to tell you in person.'

'Well. Yeah. You've done that now. So I think I'm going to go peel langoustines. Bye, Freya.'

* * *

266

On the bus home I get sent photos from an unknown number. And when I open them I see it's me with Chris.

At the bus stop earlier.

And then on the bus.

Whoever took the photos must've been sitting at the front of the top deck because there's no mistaking that it's me. Chris had his sunglasses off by then so you can see his face clearly. And he's wrapped round me.

Then comes another message.

Unknown: SLAG BAG!

I block the number.

But I know Meathead sent it.

And that means Lockie knows. He'll have seen the photos. He probably got sent the photos in the first place. And then he let Meathead do his thing. Just like last time.

Morven and Suriya must've seen the photos too. Have they? Surely Lockie would've asked them if they knew about Chris. If they knew I was meeting this *lad* when I sort-of-said I was meeting a girl from camp.

Shit! Does Lockie recognise Chris? Do they recognise him from rugby? They know Chris has an ostomy now! I told them I was meeting a friend with an ostomy. Have I just leaked Chris's private business round Lowettsons like poo making its way out below an itching, peeling, four-day-old flange? I need to find out whether they think Chris has an ostomy or not.

And Morven! This is the worst. She'll be so hurt. I straight-up lied to her this afternoon.

I message Morven once I'm home.

> **Me:** Are you free tomorrow to chat?

She replies as I'm getting ready for bed.

> **Morven:** I can come to yours for 2 p.m.

And cuddled into Winston, sniffing Nibblet, just before I fall asleep, I see Meathead's latest meme online. The same paper bag with my face on it, but with upgrades. There's poo dripping out of the bottom of the bag as well as curling out the top. And my new nickname stamped across it: SLAG BAG.

CHAPTER 32

'I've got something you're going to be excited about,' Mum says when I trail into the kitchen next morning in my dressing gown.

'What?' I say abruptly, slamming a cupboard shut.

'Take a look.' She slides a piece of paper across the kitchen counter.

Pint glass in hand, I look down at the paper. When I see who it's from, I set down the glass, lean on the counter and read the entire letter.

'Well?' she says, when I push up to standing again.

'I've decided to play hockey for school. Now.'

'This term? With your bag—?'

'Yep.'

'But that's not safe. Surely? I thought you wanted it reversed as soon as possible?'

'Yeah. Maybe I did. But it's safe to play poxy hockey

269

with an ostomy.' I go to the sink and turn on the cold tap full blast. Until I can feel it's icy cold. And fill the glass. Down half of it in one go before I top it up again. And shuffle out of the kitchen. Tossing over my shoulder, 'Book the consultation, will you? Please!' And trudge upstairs.

Back in my room I slump onto my bed and immediately regret not bringing the hospital letter with me. My surgeon's inviting me in to discuss the potential reversal of my ostomy and formation of my pouch.

I could do with speaking to Mel. But considering she warned me, '*Don't fuck Chris around*,' I'm pretty sure she won't want to give me any considered advice on the pouch.

'Is this him?' Morven says in the afternoon, peering at our canyoning team photo sitting on my dressing table.

'Yeah. Look at this one.' I hold out a copy of Chris's tuck-dive down into the water pool. 'That's him too.'

'Wow! Is he a diver?'

'I think he's lots of things . . . So they definitely just think I lied about him being from camp and having a bag?' I treble-check.

'We all did, to be honest.' Morven flushes pink. 'Suriya was livid that you'd been upset about her kissing Lockie when you're pulling someone else.' She shrugs.

'Yeah. Well. I've ruined that, now he knows Lockie and me kissed.'

'Surely if you explain Lockie and you are history then he'll understand?' She drops onto my bed and cuddles Winston.

'Don't think so. He's all about actions over words, you know?'

Morven pouts and nods. 'He's sounding better and better, Frey! Especially this outdoor shower thing. Is he into gingers . . . ?' She winks at me.

And my face crumples into ugly tears. 'Why did I kiss Lock-i-ee?'

'Oh, Frey!' She jumps up to hug me and I feel stupid for keeping secrets and blaming her for not telling me about Lockie and Suriya, because none of that matters. I'm lucky to have her. I've missed her so much.

Feeling better after we've hugged it out, I show Morven the letter from the hospital. 'Surely that's amazing news?' she says, once she's read it. 'Isn't it?' But she can see by my face that I'm not ecstatic.

'Sort of. It's not bad news. But, I don't know.'

'I thought you wanted that reversal ASAP? Isn't that what you told me in the summer?'

'Yeah . . . But my friend Mel . . .' I go retrieve the canyoning team photo. 'That's Mel there. Wait till you see this one, it's hysterical.' I show her the one of Mel death-dropping into the water pool. 'She hated me at first, but we were friends by the end.'

'Why did she hate you?'

'I might've introduced myself as Shit Bag on the first day . . .'

'To other people with bags?'

'Yeah, I'm not claiming to be the brightest highlighter in the pencil case.'

Morven frowns. 'And Chris has a bag!'

'Weirdly he was kind of into me calling myself Shit Bag. I dunno. It's like our thing now.'

'He sounds nice, Frey,' she says sadly.

'Yeah!' I sigh. 'Anyway. Mel's got *The Pouch* – the thing that stands in for your colon, remember?'

'I remember.'

'But she's considering getting rid of it and getting a permanent bag like Chris.'

Morven stares at me wide eyed. 'Why?' she says quietly.

'It's not that bad, you know. Having a bag. In some ways, it's better.'

Morven's strawberry-blonde eyebrows climb higher.

'Obviously there are loads of reasons to get rid of it. Not requiring medical apparatus for you to feel whole. Never being able to really get away from it. Especially if you want to be intimate with someone. And everyone who's *normal* will never get it. That's probably one of the reasons I've found it easier when Chris was the one I was hanging out with. He makes it feel normal to have a bag. Not abnormal. Not like my so-called *friends*. Pretty sad that everyone at school turned on me and called me Shit Bag when I'd been through all that trauma!'

There.

I've said what I thought I wouldn't dare say to her.

Morven sighs and brushes something invisible from her leg. 'We didn't want you worrying about any more of it. So we tried to deal with it in private.'

'What was private about it? It was all over social media as well as school.'

'We went to the Head. And she pulled Meathead in with his parents.'

'His mum already knew?'

'Yeah. She knew. Everyone knew. But then it was the end of term so . . . I dunno. I guess everyone just moved on. Meathead got a warning.'

'I never want to see Meathead's parents again!'

'That's fair.'

'What about Ems? She made out to Mum she didn't know Lockie started the whole thing!'

'Meathead said it was all him. You know what he's like with Lockie. And Lockie's happy to let other people take the blame. He never admits when he's in the wrong. You know that better than anyone.'

'Morv, this is so hard! Of course I *want* to get rid of my bag. When I saw all those photos of Suriya in that white bikini, I knew straight away why Lockie wanted to be with her instead of me. I want to wear bikinis! I want to be attractive!'

'You *are* attractive, Freya! That's not why Lockie did it. You know it's all about his ego. It's nothing to do with whether you're attractive or not!'

I'm crying again, ugly, snottery tears. 'But it is. Lockie thinks I'm disgusting! That's why he barely visited me in hospital. He saw my stoma through the bag and he thought it was so rank that he went with Suriya . . . and who could blame him. Suriya's stunning! I'm a fucking Shit Bag! And now Chris, the only person who'd find me attractive, doesn't like me because I'm a bad person as well as disgusting!'

Morven puffs air out. She's got tears running down her face too.

'Freya. Listen. This guy Chris and you. And your friend Mel and all the other kids who were at camp with you – none of you deserve any of this utter shit that's been dished out to you. But under no circumstances do I – or anyone else who's decent – see you as disgusting. You're the bravest, strongest, most passionate best friend a girl could ask for. And I swear to God, if Lockie ever makes you feel like you're disgusting again, I'm going to make him regret it for the rest of his life.

'And, yeah, I know I'll never truly get what it's like having a bag, but I'm trying my best to understand and educate myself. Mum told me last week that my granny who died – remember, just before my thirteenth? – she had a colostomy! Can you believe that? And I never even knew. And Mum told me this, all whispering like it was a big dirty secret. All this secrecy is bullshite! You, Frey – like Granny – are a strong woman, dealing with something really tough. And it's our job, the people around you, to step up and do better. And treat you with the respect you deserve. Because we haven't had to deal with what you have. You're the one who's better than us. Not the other way around!'

Thick tears are clouding my eyes and this time it's me giving Morven a massive hug.

'So that's today's life coaching out of the way,' she says. 'Next on the agenda – I want to hear every little detail about this kissing-in-the-outdoor-shower situation! And then we need to strategise how you're going to see Chris again.'

That night, Morven decides to stay over, and late, *late* on, we message Chris.

Me (instructed by Morven):

Me: Hey, Chris. I know this probably doesn't mean anything but I just wanted to explain that I told my ex that there was nothing between us anymore (on Thursday). The fact we kissed wasn't a good thing. But I didn't want to sound like I was making excuses when I told you yesterday. Now I've got nothing to lose, so I just wanted you to know the whole story. On Wednesday when it happened, I was crying because I'd realised that he'd been avoiding me because he'd seen my stoma in hospital. And then he kissed me. But I didn't push him away. I could have. But I didn't. But afterwards, when you and I spoke, I felt so happy and good about myself and about you, I just knew that it really was all wrong with my ex. This is done and in my past now. So I just wanted to say I'm sorry. And I miss you. But I understand that you probably won't trust me ever again. And I'll do my best to accept that. But also, I was wondering . . . would it be possible for me to borrow your support belt? That black neoprene thing. My trial's on Monday and I remember you saying that it's better to exercise with the belt on so there's less chance of my getting a hernia. And I don't have time to order one myself now. If that's possible, then let me know and maybe we could meet tomorrow. Or if you don't want to see me, maybe my friend Morven can meet you to get the belt? Shit Bag XX

P.S. I hope your godmother's party went well.
And I'm sorry about your fingers with those langoustines.

Morven can't believe I've insisted on signing it off as Shit Bag. But that's my last big hope.

In the morning there's a message waiting.

Chris: I can drop the belt round to yours before I head back to school, around 5 p.m.?

Winston muffles my screams. And I've replied before I can even tell Morven what he's said.

Me: Hey! Thank you! That would be amazing!

And I give him my address.

* * *

I'm sitting up on the landing watching the drive from 4.45 p.m. At 4.56 p.m. a black Audi turns in the gates. I run down the stairs and open the front door.

The passenger door opens while the engine's still running and Chris slips out and jogs up to the house.

'Thanks!' I say breathily.

'S'alright. Here, look.' He wraps the belt round the outside of his navy school jumper. 'You need to pull it tight. Enough that it's compressing things. But not so tight that you can't breathe or it'll stop your stoma moving. Okay?'

'Okay. Does the bag just sit below it?'

'No. Look. See that pocket . . .'

'Yeah.'

'Your bag sits inside the pocket.'

'Okay.'

The car engine stops. And Chris looks over his shoulder. The driver door opens and a tall, slim black lady with long dreads tied in a ponytail gets out. 'Mum!' Chris says, pulling off the Velcro belt.

'Don't "Mum" me, Christian. I want to meet Freya. Hi, Freya! I'm Christian's mother, Merle. I've heard a *lot* about you.'

I shake her hand. 'Hi! Pleased to meet you.' I press the doorbell to alert Mum and Dad. 'Would you like to come in for a tea or coffee?' *Please say yes!*

Merle quirks her dark eyebrows and gives me a massive,

mischievous grin. 'Why not. We don't have to be at Merchants till six. Come on, Christian, stop dandling on the doorstep.'

And she follows me inside.

We're all sitting round the kitchen table making polite chit-chat about rugby and Chris's hernia and then my hockey and stuff, and then Mum – yes, my actual mother – says, 'Why don't you go and show Chris your room for a quick five minutes, Freya?' And then she turns to Merle to check if Merle's okay with that and Merle nods to me.

'Do you want to come see my room?' I ask, heart pounding.

'Yeah . . . sure.'

Still fiddling with his support belt, I walk upstairs and Chris follows me.

'So, this is it,' I say, waving my arms wide. 'Thoughts?'

'Hmm, a bit basic.'

'What? Rude!'

'You said my boxers were basic.'

'I did. What kind have you got on today?'

Chris flicks his eyebrows as if to say, *wouldn't you like to know* . . . And tours my room with his hands tucked behind his back like he's a member of the royal family. He stops by my bed and side-nods to it. 'Who's this dude here?'

'Um. That's Winston.'

'Should I be worried about this one too?'

I suck my tongue, trying not to grin. 'Maybe . . . He does sleep with me.'

Chris drops onto my bed and lies on his hip to look Winston in his glassy bear eyes. 'Winston, man to bear, I'd like some reassurance that your intentions are honourable. Seeing as you're sharing a bed with this young . . . incredibly annoying and infuriating, but rather cute, little shitbag here.' Chris leans in closer. 'What was that, Winston?' Pretending to listen, his expressions flit from surprised, to confused, to outraged.

'What did he tell you?' I demand.

Chris shakes his head and sighs. 'Turns out you talk in your sleep.'

'Do I?'

'And you snore.'

'Do not!'

Chris sits up and shakes his head. And then bundles Winston up onto his lap. 'Yeah, mate. Course you can.' And tucks Winston under his armpit as he stands.

'Woah, woah, woah! Where are you going with my bear?'

'He wants to come with me. He wants to hang with the boys.'

I grab Winston's head. 'There's no way you're taking Winston to a smelly boys' boarding house. Winston, stay here. I promise to sleep on my side so I won't snore anymore.' We're comedy-pushing-and-pulling my giant teddy bear. 'I'll buy those plasters that rugby players wear on their noses so you can have uninterrupted slumber.'

'No one wears those anymore.'

'I will! I'll let you share my pillow and I'll relegate Nibblet to the sequinned cushion.'

'Don't listen to her, Winston,' Chris says in a panicked voice. 'It's all lies! She'll tell you what you want to hear and then she'll break your heart.'

I stop pulling. And look at Chris. 'I didn't do that . . .'

He drops Winston on my bed. 'Sorry, it was supposed to be a joke.'

'Bit too close to reality,' I murmur.

Chris reaches forward and pulls me to his chest. 'Only in parts. I appreciated your message. Your incredibly long and rambling message . . .'

I try to pull away in protest at his teasing, but Chris has me gripped. He moves my fringe with his thumb so that I can see him properly and I realise from the way he's looking at me that he's serious.

'I missed you too,' he says. 'Yesterday I wanted to tell all my family about you and every time I started to say something, I remembered I'd walked away and left you.'

I lean into his chest and hug him tight.

He rubs my back. And then says, 'Can we kiss now, please? Because I think I'm going to have to go back to school soon.'

'Oh yeah.'

He sits, pulls me onto his knee and wraps his arms around me. 'Hello, Shit Bag,' he says, his nose touching mine.

'Hello,' I whisper.

He nudges my nose and kisses my top lip softly.

Bundled in Chris's arms, I'm too impatient. I move my hand out so he releases it and I slide it up round the back of his neck, tickling his skin as I pass, and then I pull his head down closer to me, and I kiss him firmly, deeply. Our lips, tongues, breath, fingers, skin. We end up shifting onto my bed so that we're lying and I feel the weight of his body. Absorbed. With ourselves.

Until we hear his mum call from downstairs.

And we both sit up, flustered and rumpled.

'Coming!' Chris shouts.

I walk to my mirror and wipe my smudged mascara. Smooth down my hair.

'I might have to empty my bag before I go. Is that okay?' he says.

'Course,' I say. 'Bathroom's next door. I'll go down and tell them.'

'Wait. Can I ask you something first?'

I move to him again, and because he's still sitting, I wrap my arms around his neck. 'You may.'

'Thank you.' He grins. And then says, 'Is this Nibblet?' And he's holding up my dilapidated stuffed rabbit.

'Yes,' I squeak.

'Is Nibblet a girl?'

'Yes. She is.'

'Can Nibblet come to school with me?'

'No!'

'Please! I have my own accessible study bedsit. It's really nice. It has an en suite shower room. I don't share with a roommate and I have a locker in the room. I could lock her up through the day so no one touches her.'

'You want to lock my most precious possession in a cupboard all day?'

He grimaces. 'Yeah, when you say it like that . . .'

'Why do you want to take her?'

'I want to be able to think of you when I'm in bed, and smell you . . .'

I blink. 'That's both thrilling and a bit stalker in one.'

'I'd rather it wasn't stalker.'

'Christian!' Chris's mum shouts.

I say in a rush, 'When can I have her back?'

His face lights up. 'The next time we see each other?'

'Okay. But you have to guard her with your life!' And I kiss him slowly on his forehead, nose, right cheek, left cheek and then on his perfect mouth, so *so* deep that he falls backwards onto my bed . . . and I run downstairs.

CHAPTER 33

I'm high on life!

So when I see Meathead in the common room first thing Monday morning, I send a quick message to Chris to double-check something and once I've got my answer back, I saunter over to have a wee chat. Shit Bag (Slag Bag) v Meathead.

'Morning, Meathead,' I say brightly. 'Have a good weekend?'

'What do you want, slag?'

'Why so angry, Meathead? You not feeling well?'

'I'm angry 'cause you're pulling Christian Blair. Why're you messing around with Lockie like that?'

I knew he'd recognised Chris.

'You a druggy too? You and him look like you're junkie extras off that *Trainspotting* film. That lad used to be a rugby legend – total waste.'

Technically Chris *is* on drugs – prescription drugs – but

I'm definitely not telling Meathead that truth. 'You do seem out of sorts, Meathead. You sure you're feeling okay? You're acting a bit . . . constipated. You might want to watch that. Take my advice. Keeping that anger inside . . . you'll end up with gut problems like me.'

'What do you mean?'

'Well, you know that's what happened to Chris, right?'

'What?'

'Being a sporting *legend* – and, well, he's not angry but you are, and being angry, that'll do it too – that's why Chris has got a *shit bag* like me. Didn't Lockie tell you? I told him I was meeting a friend from camp.'

'Yeah, but you lied.'

'No. Chris has got a shit bag *just like me*. So, word of advice, you'd better watch out for the symptoms. So you don't end up like us . . .' I turn and walk away.

'Wait! What are the symptoms?'

I wave bye over my shoulder.

But then he shouts after me, 'You know, Lockie doesn't care anyway! He met up with Imogen Watson yesterday. They've been pulling since Easter. He never wanted you after you got that shit bag!'

My heart's racing at that piece of news. What an absolute arsehole Lockie is. No wonder Imogen was gunning for me. And the most significant element in that last firing shot from Meathead is that I didn't even have my ostomy at Easter, we were just arguing back then. So my shit bag is just another excuse. Another reason, in a very long list, why Lockie and I should've ended it ages ago.

When Suriya and Morven arrive in school, I take them somewhere quiet and I tell Suriya about Imogen. She takes it stoically. Then admits she saw him with Imogen the week before autumn term started. She insists she's fine. That he's a dick. And she's glad she made Imogen cry for the incident in the dining room.

I also tell Suriya who the guy was that I was with on Friday. How we know each other. How I'll introduce them to him soon. That we're officially a couple and I'm really happy.

That Chris's bag is permanent and that's a lot to unpack for me as well as other people. But he's going to try and get back to playing rugby when his hernia's healed and his Crohn's has calmed down.

And, yeah, I'm definitely trialling for the hockey team today and if I do really shit, at least I've tried.

I tell them they're amazing and I'm grateful to have them both as friends.

They hug *me*.

And *we* hug Suriya.

CHAPTER 34

I should be out on the pitches right now and instead I'm sitting in a cubicle in the loos, beside the old wood-panelled gym in the main school. The window above me is open, so I can hear some of the hockey squad shouting, warming up. I've already changed into my games kit. I couldn't face the rest of the team in the main changing rooms. I didn't want them all gawking at my bag, not while I was trying to get my head literally in the game.

That might be a lucky coincidence because as I was heading along the corridor outside, I scratched my flange. Because it was itchy.

I hear a whistle and Ms Jarvis shouts for the whole of the squad outside. I chew and swallow the marshmallow in my mouth rather than spit it out, but just like it did a moment ago, the chewing makes my stoma move again. Not that helpful considering I'm sitting here completely *sans* bag-and-flange, because a leak worked its way out under the flange. And with my pink-and-yellow – Hard Boiled Sweets – sports top tucked up out of the way, under my chin. Guess this is just one of those days, weeks, years!

I wipe away the poo and drop the tissue into the pan and press another clean piece of loo roll over the top of my stoma. *Stay there, please!* Thank God Chris suggested I pre-cut the stoma hole in my emergency flanges. If I had to cut a hole at the right size for my stoma right now, with my hands shaking like this, I'd be in tears. Instead, I'm just trying to keep calm. In control, in an itsy-bitsy crisis.

I lay my already clipped bag out over my leg, peel the backing paper from the flange and apply the paste around the hole. Then I breathe in and out, relaxed, wait to check that I haven't induced more movement, and quickly wipe my stoma again, stick the flange over the top, press it down as firmly as possible without pushing too hard on my stomach, grab the bag and fix it over the top of the flange, locking the catch to tighten its seal and connection.

Right.

I shove all the little bits into the scented nappy sack, cram it in the 'feminine hygiene bin', flush and go out to wash my hands.

This isn't me sorted though.

It usually takes an hour before the sticky back of the flange really adheres to my skin. And that's skin that's not sweating buckets because it's playing hockey for the first time since the stoma's creation. I pause, looking at myself in the mirror. And remember the electrical tape and how Chris used it to keep his bag on once. I rifle through my emergency kit again and wrap a criss-cross of blue tape across my stomach like a reverse Scottish saltire, making contact over the top and bottom ribbed disc edges of the flange. That'll have to do. I strap on the Velcro neoprene support belt that I borrowed from Chris, and run outside.

'Great to have you back, Freya,' Sarah our captain says, high-fiving me in the main changing room after the trial.

Emily, the Upper Six Left Wing, holds her hand up for me to high-five it too. 'I liked that set-up in the last ten. You'll have to teach me it.'

I slap her palm and grin. That was a trick shot I watched on YouTube.

I wrap my towel round my waist and do my best to wriggle my soaked games shirt off without dislodging my makeshift privacy shield. I've been buzzing with adrenaline since we entered the changing rooms, and only now have I realised that I need to get myself into a shower without any of them seeing my bag. And what happens when I come out of the shower?

And actually, I need to empty it.

And I think I've got welts on my ribs and hips because of the electrical tape. Chris's idea might work for watching sport on the sidelines but it's not ideal for actually playing sport. Because it doesn't stretch. At times it felt like playing hockey in a corset.

I pull the towel up over my sports bra, grab my toilet bag and wander through to the loos.

I manage to peel the reverse saltire off without taking too much skin with it – there are blood-blister bruise marks on both ribs but hey-ho. The flange seems to have stayed in place with no suspect itchiness as yet. I'm a winner!

I empty my bag, light a match and spray air freshener, then decide that, even though it's soaking wet from sweat, I'm going to just keep Chris's support belt on over the bag. That way, if anyone catches a glimpse all they'll see is the black neoprene guard – acceptably sporty-looking. So I wriggle sedately under my towel, out of my remaining clothes and get into a shower cubicle. Obviously the belt's absolutely sopping wet after my shower, which isn't ideal.

Back with the others, I manage to get my bra and pants on while still wearing my towel. I'm an arm into my school shirt when I just stop. A light going on in my head. *Finally*, I appreciate how far I've come. I'm being an idiot. No one's really even looking at me. Well, maybe they're glancing. But we all do that when we're changing. Worrying about how we look to each other and trying to get our clothes on fast without seeming self-conscious. I know I'm not ready to show them *all of it*, up close and personal: my scar, bag and flange. Not yet. But that's my choice. My privilege. Maybe I'll *never* show them my stoma! That's up to me. But, all the same, I don't need to act like I have a dirty little secret under here either. Like Morven said her granny felt she had to hide her ostomy's existence.

So I take my first step towards public acceptance and rip off Chris's neoprene belt, drop it on the ground, and dry all around my stomach, over my scar and below my bag so it won't turn into a damp itch-fest on the way home. And only when I'm dry enough do I pull on my shirt and the rest of my uniform like I've always done.

All packed up, I realise that no one has gone home yet. They're all sat chatting and laughing. So I stay too. And it feels like coming home. Finally. Chris was right. I have missed being able to play my sport. Being part of my team. And even if I don't get to play a game this season, I'm still part of the squad. I don't feel as lost and lonely as I have for months.

'Okay, everyone!' Sarah shouts, clapping her hands. 'Thanks for staying behind! Okay . . . !' She waits for all the talking to die down. 'I just want to say well done. That was a really nice session tonight. Clearly everyone learned just as much hockey in Portugal as they enjoyed getting up to mischief. So I'm really excited to see how our season plays out this year.' She starts clapping. Everyone else follows suit and I do the same, despite feeling very much not part of what she's just said.

'Brilliant. So the real reason we're here now is because one of us didn't make it to training camp. She missed out on all the revelry that got us in trouble, as well as the team-bonding and fitness. And instead, she went through something that – we're all in agreement on this, yes?' She waits for the reply.

And is met with 'YES!' 'Absolutely!' 'Sheeeesh!'

Before she continues, 'Something that none of us could've handled – certainly in no way as stoically as she has!'

This is followed with *yelps* and *woo hoos*.

'Freya! You did yourself proud tonight! After everything you've been through, you still competed technically and physically. You're the strongest girl we know. We salute you! We're in awe and we're just plain glad to have you back among us. Here's to a great season ahead, team, and here's to Freya!'

'FREYA! FREY-YA! FREY-YA!' everyone shouts, and suddenly the whole squad comes up, hugging me and squeezing me and saying really lovely things about how happy they are that I'm here. And Suriya even says she loves me. And Morven says all the kind things I'd expect from her but it's still special to hear anyway.

But then something really unexpected happens. A girl called Minn asks across the changing room, 'Freya? Would it be okay if we have a chat sometime about your bag? It's just my aunt has one and she refuses to talk about it. I was just thinking if I knew a bit more, maybe I could start a conversation with her about it . . . ?'

'My grandpa's got one,' someone else says.

'Sure,' I say. 'Ask whatever you want. I'll tell you what I can.'

'I have a question,' Emma, our goalie, says. 'Will you have your bag for the rest of your life?' There's a rumble of agreement, as if they've all wondered that. I guess it's the obvious question.

I'm honest and lay out the facts. 'I don't know yet. I haven't decided. It's up to me what happens, and I haven't really lived with it long enough to know whether I prefer it or if I'm prepared to give it up and maybe lose the freedom it's giving me just now.'

There's understandably a bit of confusion when I say this. It took me long enough to get my head around what Mel was, and still is, telling me. That it's not all fairy tales and rainbows when you get your pouch. But I know that talking about the pouch isn't what this lot need to hear

293

right now. I feel like I'm the PR ambassador for ostomies and I need to explain this right.

'What I'm trying to say is, an ostomy bag can save your life.' They all nod, getting that. 'But I might *keep* mine because it saves my *lifestyle*. It's my choice. Not just a last resort – it's not forced on me. It's actually *desirable*!' Yeah, that last part has pickled their brains.

They all start talking at once, firing more questions. Thankfully, Sarah spots that it's getting a bit much for me and suggests a team Q&A in a couple of weeks.

Then Minn says, 'I wish my aunt had such an open mind. But hers is permanent, I think.'

I pause before I speak, but then decide, *fuck it, I'm going in*.

'The guy I'm seeing has a permanent ostomy. I know he'd be okay with me sharing that he's planning on playing rugby for Merchants First Fifteen with his permanent ostomy.'

And it kicks off. 'What?'

'Who . . . ?'

'What happened to Lockie?'

'Who in Merchants Firsts has a bag?'

I can't speak. I'm laughing and blushing in one. That's like the ultimate Edinburgh Schools mic drop. *Boom!*

Chris said he had nothing to hide when I asked him this morning, before I approached Meathead, so I know he's cool with people knowing, but still . . .

'Come on, Freya, spill!'

I exchange knowing smiles with Morven and Suriya. I feel like I've come so far over the last two months. So much has moved on. 'So,' I say, and they all shush and fall silent, 'it's Chris – Christian – Blair. Do you know him?'

'What?'

'You are fucking joking!'

'I heard he was going back a year. Is that why? Because he's got a bag?'

'*Now* I've got questions. I've got loads of questions!'

'Can Chris come do the Q&A too?'

'Yeah, Freya, maybe Chris can be your live model and demonstrate . . . ?'

'Let's do a dual team talk! Let's do a Merchants Firsts rugby with Lowettsons Firsts Girls hockey, all together!'

I hide my face in my hands and laugh, and in this perfect moment I resolve that I do have a choice.

The choice to decide what happens in my life and with my body. Based entirely on how I feel. Today and in the future.

Not based on what my family and friends, ex-friends, boyfriends, surgeons or the world at large think is *normal*. Or disgusting or weird.

No. If I decide to keep my ostomy bag it'll be because it makes my life easier. And that doesn't make me Shit Bag.

That makes me Freya.

Acknowledgements

This book was a long time to publication – it's been a glorious journey of discovery.

I found my writing voice slowly and later in life, attending a variety of writing courses and coaching.

Specifically, I'd like to thank City Lit adult education college in London for teaching me the grammar and punctuation I didn't understand at school. Also at City Lit – Gavin Campbell my TV Presenting tutor for being the first person to tell me I was 'rather good at writing' – this was a revelation! English had always been something I'd struggled with.

Thanks to author and mentor Daren King. I found my own writing style under Daren's gentle novel mentoring, and I always carry with me his top writing tip: to finish on the most important word.

Thanks too to author and tutor Anthony McGowan for encouraging my embryonic idea of a YA story about a teenage girl with an ostomy bag with the title of *Shit Bag!* (It's always the titles that come first for me.) And for teaching me about punctums – painting such a pinpoint image in the reader's mind that it lingers.

And then to SCBWI for providing a supportive, bright and positive environment to meet fellow children's authors.

Through SCBWI, I found my author critique group – the KC Criterati. Now evolved into a life (and literary) support group. It was in the early days of our critique meetings that *SH!T BAG* transformed from a mere title into a novel that would get me a literary agent. With the steady, wise, nurturing, confident and instinctive insights provided by these special, and incredibly talented, women and their daughters – A.M. Dassu (Az), Annie Harris, Ella Harris, Camilla Chester, Fay Chester, N.M. Browne, Sarah Day, Eliza Day and Sue Wallman – I developed as an author, flourished and believed.

And it was thanks to a SCBWI agents party, I met my amazing agent Jo Williamson of Antony Harwood Literary Agency. There are too many reasons and need for me to thank Jo. But to sum things up here briefly – she is my voice of reason, she is my champion, my ally in strategy and negotiation and my friend, to chat about fun things like parties, rugby and horseracing . . . Thank you, always, Jo!

And now to Harriet Wilson. This novel would not exist without Harriet. Harriet, this is all you!

You read *SH!T BAG* way back in 2017 and held it with you until the time was right, and the publishing house was right, to do it justice. In your role as Publisher, Fiction Brands & Classics at Hachette Children's Group, as my editor, and on a personal level, thank you for empowering me and understanding me. Thank you for *getting* me. Getting Freya!

Georgina Mitchell, thank you, along with Harriet, for your editorial support and guidance, advice, insights, ideas and endorsement of my message.

SH!T BAG has developed and changed throughout this editorial process so that I'm really proud of what we've achieved together as a team. But equally, I've learned so much in your care and light-touch expertise, about myself as a writer, how my brain works, about my 'style and voice', improving, growing, navigating this new world of publishing. At times this has been a fast and furious ride. But I've loved the whole journey!

And to the wider team at Hachette Children's Group – Joana Reis, the cover designer, for catching Freya perfectly, Marketing, PR, Rights . . . line and copy editors, proofreaders . . . the list goes on. Because I'm humbled yet energised, and still very emotional that this dream has become a reality. Thank you for your hard work, excitement and championing. We are bigger and better working together. And I can't wait for *SH!T BAG* – and Freya – to be out in the world because of you ALL!

And in my personal life:

My parents, siblings, family and friends who've supported me over the years. And got me through those nights, days and years of illness, physical weakness, building me up, enduring my fiery frustrations, my 'unique' personality . . . getting me back bigger and better to where I am now – all of the things that inspired and fuelled this novel. And gave me insight into my characters, Freya and the rest, who are raw and real in their own flawed ways. Thanks!

To my husband, Iain. Thanks for being my partner! In everything we do.

Re SH!T BAG – thanks for making the right noises and providing a human-shaped sounding-wall, and special insight into a teenage rugby lad's mind. We have a routine where I speak *at* you, you answer a question or provide a suggestion under time pressure and then good naturedly sit there waiting (as long as it only takes a couple of minutes!) while I say – 'no, that's crap . . . but what about this?'. I make light of our process, but it's helped me work through so many plot or character-building problems, that my writing would be so much weaker without you. Because I am more *me* with you beside me!

And finally, I'm grateful and give thanks to myself. I was alone inside my body through those dark nights in hospital, surgery, recovery, missing ordinary socialising, no longer a carefree late-teen and ever-since throughout life there's always been something to battle . . . This shitty dysfunctional gut of mine (and more) has tested me. But that's life! And I'm grateful for who I am. It's my personality, strength, stoicism, humour and tenacity that have got me here. I'm bold. Angry at times. Passionate. Sensitive. Self-deprecating. Perhaps a bit arrogant . . . ? Flawed, certainly. But I'm proud that I've kept going. And that's all we can really do in life, in my view.

So, I'll pat myself on the back, if you promise to do the same. Because we're all just dealing with our own shit!